One against the Infidels!

At the crest of a Lebanon hill, a lone rider sat his great black war horse and gazed down grimly at the miniature battle raging beneath him.

A dozen Saracens in gleaming mail whipped around three figures on the knoll, curved scimitars golden in the sunlight. John of Lincoln knew the Saracen kind, and in return they knew John of Lincoln—and his great spiked ball.

But it was the woman who held him motionless in the saddle. The woman in rich brocaded riding clothes, guarded by two swarthy men-at-arms, the woman whose eyes glittered over a veil of thin black silk, the woman who fought with strange, foreign weapons but killed as expertly as any man.

John of Lincoln admired courage, even pagan courage. He lifted his battle cry into the hot Syrian air, dug his golden spurs into his barded horse, and careened down the sloping hill.

The spiked iron ball was whirling rapidly, screaming shrilly now. He drove in among the Seljuks and the iron ball came down and round in a mighty sweep. Two men died as those long metal spikes bit deep into their faces.

As he fought he shouted the Templar battle cry. *"Bauceant! Bauceant!"* And as he swung the spiked ball he mocked them: "Taste the kiss of the whirling devil! No houri of paradise offers the ecstasy she can bring you! Only once may a man taste *her* caress!"

ONE SWORD
FOR LOVE

Gardner F. Fox

WILDSIDE PRESS

FOREWORD

There are a few yellowing pages of an eight-hundred-year-old letter now on display in the British Museum. Those eight pages, and the ten that may be seen in Vienna, and the others at Munich and in the library of Paris, were written by a man whom time has labeled a myth.

The fact that a German bishop has also written of this man, and that Pope Alexander III chose to write to him, would seem to add weight to the question of his actuality. World scholars and travelers like Maimonides and Marco Polo, Juan de Plane Carpini and Sir John Mandeville, wrote of and believed in this strange man-myth who styled himself Prester John.

Truth is an elusive needle in a historical haystack The only facts that emerge from the flowery letters and the scholarly writings are these: that a medieval Christian knight rose to power somewhere in middle Asia during the twelfth century, and that he roused up the nomadic hordes of the steppe country in a great Asiatic crusade designed to sweep the Holy Land from the grip of the Seljuk Turks and Moslems, who were then disputing its ownership with the Crusaders.

Eight hundred years ago, less was known about inner Asia than is known about the moon today. A century after these letters by pope and bishop were written, Marco Polo was to travel to far Cathay. Some years before that time, a conqueror called Genghis Khan brought those same nomad hordes out of middle Asia on his own personal crusade for power. There where Marco Polo and Genghis Kahn rode, rode also Prester John.

Who was this man, this Prester John? If he was a real person, as seems probable, how did he come to the plains of Kara-Khitai? What inheritance of fate brought him to an Asiatic throne?

It is with some hope of clothing this mythical man with the fictional flesh of reality, and in the belief that this is the way it could have happened, that I give you Sir John, an English knight from the fen country of Lincolnshire, and the veiled woman he knew as Shirzade.

GARDNER F. FOX

ONE SWORD
FOR LOVE

Chapter One

A DEAD MAN lay at the side of the limestone road that wound through the hills of Lebanon. His thin, dark face was framed under a steel helmet wrapped about by a white cloth *ogal*. His hand, upturned in death, still held the hilt of a curved scimitar whose blade was snapped in half. Another dead man, in striped *jelab* over ring-mail armor, lay beyond him, and beyond that man, another. The dead men left a trail from the limestone road to a high hill where a frankincense tree stirred bare branches against the hot wind.

A lone horseman on the limestone road frowned down at the dead Saracen. He was a big man in silvery chain mail under a white surcoat that was emblazoned with a large red cross. A flat helm, from which fell a collar of interwoven links, gave him the appearance of an iron man. His wide, sensitive mouth was set under a slightly jutting jaw tinted almost copper from six years of fighting in this Syrian sunlight.

The rider came down out of the high wooden saddle and knelt beside the first dead man. He put a hand on the short black shaft that protruded from the Moslem's throat and tugged it free, his hard gray eyes studying the broad steel point and the cut of the feathers.

He turned the arrow over and over in his fingers, his yellow brows drawn together in puzzlement. John of Lincoln had never seen an arrow like this one, with its lacquered shaft and those odd black feathers. He went to his war horse and, loosening the strap that held the worn leather saddlebag at the high, curved pommel, tied the arrow to it. Then he swung his mailed body up into the saddle and toed the stallion forward.

He found two more dead Saracens in a little gully, each of them dead of those short, black shafts. More of them lay huddled on the slope of a hill beyond the row of poplars bordering the road.

"No Turk or Arab fires such an arrow," he told the chain collar that hung at his throat. "No Christian knight, either."

His duty was to gallop back along the limestone road that stretched between these craggy hills to the Buqaia River, where it turned south and west to the coastal city of Tripolis. Some miles behind him the Lady Hodierna, sister to Melisande, queen of Jerusalem, impatiently awaited his return.

John of Lincoln grimaced. Her soft red mouth would lash him mercilessly, reminding him of his duty to the wife of Raymond, Count of Tripolis. And she would stir and move her rounded legs and arms, and twist that curving torso, smiling boldly up at him with her hot blue eyes to challenge his manhood.

"Hai," he muttered into the wind. "She will tell me in many ways that it is my duty to escort her to the Krak."

The Krak of the Knights was the powerful Crusader fortress whose stone bulk guarded the mountain passes of Lebanon from the attacks of Saracen raiders in this year of Christ 1141. John of Lincoln was riding there to take command in the name of Raymond, to fly the red and yellow banner of Tripolis above its score of towers.

For over forty years the Holy Land had been safely in

the mailed hands of the Crusaders. Godfrey of Bouillon
lay buried in a sarcophagus at Calvary, as Baldwin lay
at Golgotha. The kingdom these men had begun at Antioch and Ascalon still was strong and robust, but cracks
in that armed façade were already appearing. Quarrels
between the proud Crusader lords were undermining the
united front that had swept the Musselmen out of the
coastal strip of the Holy Land, leaving it full of treachery
and mistrust. To further their own ends, certain Frankish
rulers were rumored to be making treaties with their
Moslem enemies.

Moreover, the Saracens were uniting under a Seljuk
Turk, Imadeddin Zengi, who was gathering the Moslem
strength and directing the eyes of all True Believers
toward the Holy Land. To harass the infidels, the Seljuks
often made swift forays into Lebanon.

John of Lincoln knew that these dead men formed part
of such a raiding force. He knew that it was his duty first
to consider the safety of the Lady Hodierna in these
troubled times; but that black shaft drew him with the
odd fascination of a magical incantation.

He must learn what manner of men fired those strange
arrows with the wide steel points. Let the Countess rage
as she would, he meant to see those archers for himself!
His lips thinned to a hard line, the Crusader spurred his
black horse up the sloping hill, and past the tall poplars,
riding hard.

As he swayed in the high-cantled wooden saddle, his
right hand fumbled at his knee, where a mace-and-chain
hung over a wooden pommel peg. He lifted the short
chain and the large spiked iron ball by its horn handle,
which had turned black with much use. He swung the
ball over his head twice, and the sound of its passing
made an eerie whistle in the air. There were thin passages
bored through the solid iron, and the wind whirling
through them came out screaming.

The crest of the hill was bare, its ancient red clay lit-
tered with cracked boulders and broken marl. From its
height the lone rider could look down into a natural
bowllike valley half a mile wide, where a single low
mound, covered with cracked stone and rock slag, was
set almost in its middle.

A dozen Saracens in striped jelabs and gleaming mail
crowded around three figures on the knoll, curved scimi-

tars bright and golden in the sunlight. John of Lincoln knew their kind. He had fought with them at Montferrand and Balat, and only recently at Niksar. In turn, he reflected grimly, the paynims knew John of Lincoln and his great spiked ball.

But it was the three figures fighting the Moslems that caught and held the Crusader momentarily motionless in the saddle. Two of them were short men with swart faces under leather caps trimmed in fur, and clad in black sheepskins over lacquered leather armor. They fought with curving swords and strange, two-hafted daggers called katars. On their left arms they wore round shields of bullhide, varnished and strengthened by bands of red copper and bossed with iron.

The third figure was that of a woman. She wore brocaded riding trousers stitched with red leather that fitted her tightly from her thighs down to her knees, where they were slit to flare wide apart, revealing dusty red leather boots. A short brocaded coat was belted at her slim waist by a girdle of golden disks. Over her face, where it was not shadowed by her woolen cloak, a thin yashmak, or veil of black silk, fluttered to her movements.

The woman fought with a scimitar as did the men; but instead of a round shield, she held two twisted lengths of black horn, fitted together with a space for gripping fingers. John of Lincoln watched the woman move the hand shield here and there expertly, and as the hard horn deflected the Seljuk blades, her own scimitar thrust hard.

The Crusader admired bravery, even pagan bravery. He lifted his battle cry into the hot Syrian air, and his mace-and-chain began to rotate faster and faster. He dug his golden prick spurs into his horse and careened down the hill. The spiked iron ball was whirling rapidly now, screaming shrilly. He drove in among the Seljuks and the iron ball came down and around in a mighty sweep. Two men died as those long metal spikes bit deep into their faces.

As he fought, he shouted the Templar battle cry: "*Bauceant! Bauceant!*"

He handled the chained ball as though it were an extra fist. It went out to a man and brained him, then darted sideways to plunge long spikes into a throat or an eye;

then danced lightly, with the grace of a skimming bird, to fell a third by crushing his high spiked helmet in its turban wrapping.

As he swung the spiked ball, he mocked them. "Taste the kiss of the whirling devil! No houri of paradise offers the ecstasy she can bring you. Only once may a man taste *her* caress!"

They knew this mad rider and his whistling weapon. Hai, how they knew him! They had faced him at Aleppo, and on the coastal plains of Tripolis, when his flailing mace had smashed a path for Count Raymond's father to flee to the mountains.

Their curved scimitars lifted and swung, but were snapped in two by the flying ball. They rushed him, jelabs flying, but the mace came to meet them, caving in chests and ribs, puncturing their grooved mail as though it were wet vellum.

The black war horse had been trained in the palace fields at Jerusalem for this work. His great shod hoofs lifted as he reared, then lashed out at paynim faces. His blasting trumpet echoed the whistling scream of the thudding mace.

They fought madly, these Saracens, with passion twisting their dark faces. But they could find no way to stop that hurtling spiked ball; and so, sullenly, they withdrew.

The Crusader watched them go, resting his mace arm across the high pommel of his wooden saddle. As he had thought, they were just a raiding band of Seljuks sweeping in over the Lebanese border for what they could snatch of Christian treasure or Christian women with skins the color of fresh milk.

It was the others that commanded his attention. He sighed and turned toward the trousered woman with the veil and the small archers who had been defending her. But the little rise of rocky ground where they had fought was empty. They had disappeared as ruins disappear before the encrouching advance of wind-blown sands.

Gratitude is never one of their virtues, the Templar thought wryly.

He could see them in the distance, galloping on shaggy ponies past a high stone hummock that lifted lean and jagged from the level of the valley floor. Lacquered bow cases and quivers were slung on their hips, on either side of their black barracans.

The woman straddled a big bay horse with black mane and tail. John of Lincoln knew a sudden restless desire to withdraw the silk veil that sheathed the lower part of her face. He wondered whether her features resembled the fat moon faces of the paynim women who worshiped in the Aksa mosque, below the Dome of the Rock and above the royal palace at Jerusalem, or the soft oval loveliness of the houris that Mohammed taught his followers waited to welcome them to paradise.

The black war horse shook his head with a jingle of the armorial pendants attached to his chest straps. The Crusader leaned forward, patting the thick glossy neck.

"We ride, Thane. And we ride fast, lest the Lady Hodierna vent the spleen of her temper on us, as we've seen her do to others who displeased her!"

He put the fight behind him, for he was used to these border skirmishes. But he was aware of a vague, dissatisfied regret in him that he used the mace only in these futile little forays. If only he fought in some mightier battle, where he might, like Godfrey and Baldwin of the Mount, stand alone on Jerusalem's wall to hold off the Musselmen while the scaling ladders were lifted!

John of Lincoln conceived himself born a generation too late. The Holy Land, which had passed from Arab to Seljuk Turk in 1076, and from Seljuk Turk to Crusader twenty years later, was now safely in Christian hands. From Tortosa and Antioch in the north, the coastal cities of Tripolis and Beirut and Jerusalem itself, flew the Crusader banners.

There was no path now where a man with a weapon might hew out a monument to his faith. The Holy Sepulcher was in Frankish hands. The Cross flew over the towers of Acre and Beirut. Only in the lands beyond the thin strip of coastline, beyond the Sea of Galilee and the Jordan, were there paynim cities. And no man in his right mind cared who held those hot desert lands.

Glumly John of Lincoln removed his iron helm with its attached collar of mail. He hung it at his pommel above the straps that held the black lacquered arrow, and rode with his poll naked to the air, pale yellow hair cropped close in the Templar fashion.

He moved up the hill to the frankincense tree, and down the far slope to the limestone road where the poplars grew. He put the black stallion to a canter, aware

that the Countess of Tripolis would be angry at his long
absence.

Two miles below the band of the road where the dead
Saracens lay, he came upon a litter. It was an ornate
thing, its sturdy frame and wooden poles coated with blue
paint. The wheels were tall, colored blue and crimson,
and where the carved poles held the flat canopy, silken
curtains were drawn back to reveal tufted cushions.

The Countess stood before it, regal and haughty, her
chin upheld proudly as she scanned the bare brown hills.
She wore a *bliaud* of blue silk that fitted tightly at shoulder and bosom down to wide hips, where it fell in graceful folds to her slippered feet. A girdle of thin silver rings
bound her slim waist. On her head, against the Lebanon
heat, she wore a wimple of white silk fitted with a blue
velvet toque. A great square emerald glittered on her
forefinger.

That she was angry the Lady Hodierna revealed in the
studied disdain with which she ignored John of Lincoln
as he reined his war horse to a halt. She moved a shoulder
petulantly, and her thin, aristocratic nostrils flared to the
temper that made her blue eyes blaze.

"I found this, milady," he explained, bending from the
saddle to show her the lacquered arrow shaft. "A strange
arrow fired by small men whose like I have never seen."

He went on with his explanation, revealing the presence of the swart men and the veiled woman. "The paynims attacked them. They are their enemies, then, as
well as ours. I have been considering a possible search
party, that we may seek them out and have words with
them. An alliance would be a good thing."

"You have been considering an alliance, messire? You
ought only to have been considering my safety!"

She looked at him now, and there was more than anger
in the blue eyes that sought his face. Her hands came
together. "We are few, Sir John. Only a handful of men
at arms. We are near the Krak. And where the Krak is,
there are the pagans. It might have been me trying to
defend myself as you tell me that trousered woman defended herself."

The Lady Hodierna seemed faint at the very thought.
She touched the back of her hand to her forehead, push-
ing back the wimple so that a few strands of thick chestnut hair slid out to caress her soft cheek.

It was the signal for John of Lincoln to make amends. He swung down and put a mailed arm about her shoulders. It seemed to him that the Lady Hodierna leaned more heavily against him than her malaise warranted. He felt the rondure of an ungirdled hip on his, and the touch of a soft thigh.

Her white, ringed hand clasped and held his fingers. From the pillow of his chest her lovely face smiled up at him.

"Sir John! Sir John! How you try our patience!" she sighed.

"Forgive me then, milady. It was only the thought of your safety that sent me over the hill. I wanted to see the paynims, and the numbers of the strange little men with the black arrows."

She caught at the solace he offered, and her soft fingers squeezed his hand. "If I could believe it was my safety that was your main concern! You are so hard, so st. ng! Like a man of iron in all that mail, with that sword at your belt, and that horrible spiked ball on your saddle!"

He smiled uneasily. She could not know how she affected him, with her sweet perfumed flesh that was so disturbingly soft and yielding. She could not realize how the wind pressed her silken *bliaud* against her body.

"Assist me, messire," she directed, and contrived so to walk against him that his face was flushed as he handed her into the curtained litter.

Her laughter mocked him gently as she lay back among the cushions. The Lady Hodierna was a fleshly woman, with the full breasts of recent motherhood. Her ample hips and dark complexion were inherited from the Armenian princess who had been her mother. There was a languorous quality to her large dark eyes and moist red mouth, and the scented brown hair she displayed with such artful disarrangement under the silken folds of her wimple was thick and heavy. Sensual and arrogant, she let her heavy lips droop into a smile as her hungry eyes drank in the mailed form of John of Lincoln. His hair was flaxen, glowing in the Syrian sunlight. He was a pleasure to the eyes, this big knight, and the Lady Hodierna congratulated herself on her discernment. His presence was a relief from the boredom that had plagued her in the gardens of her Tripolitan palace.

"You are courteous, messire, not to reproach me for

my unjust criticisms. My concern was more for your safety than my own."

Her ringed fingers gestured at the escort that flanked the limestone road behind her, indicating that the men at arms her husband had furnished were more than a match for any raiding Saracens.

John of Lincoln bowed his head in acknowledgment. He was not used to women, and he was finding the Countess of Tripolis a disturbing distraction to eyes that should be alert for danger.

That the Lady Hodierna was aware of his distraction was evidenced by the smile on her wide mouth. She lay back, flaunting herself at his gray eyes, toying with the girdle of silver rings at her waist.

"You will ride beside me, to keep me company for the remainder of our journey, Sir John. There are certain matters I would speak of that only your ears should hear."

Despite the languor in her eyes, her request was an order. John of Lincoln waved two men at arms forward at the gallop, then swung the black war horse in beside the litter.

They paced slowly through these barren hills, flanked to the east by the vast red desert stretching from the Orontes as far as the Euphrates. Southward lay the mountains of Lebanon, and beyond them the Sea of Galilee. Behind them was the coast, and the blue waters of the Mediterranean.

They paced through this coastal plain, known to the Crusaders as La Bocquee, through which flowed the waters of the Nahr-el-Kebir. Like a wedge between the mountains, it formed an arrow at the heart of the Frankish midkingdoms. To guard this vital passage between the natural mountain barriers, great stone fortresses had been built: Arima and Akkar in the Lebanons, and beyond them the mighty ramparts of the Krak of the Knights.

It was the Krak that was their destination, John of Lincoln riding to command its garrison and its massive walls, the Lady Hodierna to further her own interest, under the pretext of a holiday in the dry inland regions.

The sun was warm on his coat of ring mail, and on the mailed *chausses* on his legs, but it was not the heat of the sun so much as the dark eyes of the Lady Hodierna that made the Crusader squirm in his big wooden saddle.

The mocking smile on that red mouth and the occasional sigh with which she drew his eyes to her as she turned on the brocaded cushions of the litter added fuel to the inner warmth that was bringing a film of sweat to his brow.

"You are no longer a Templar, Sir John," she reminded him, as they moved through a dry wadi dotted with thorn scrub. Her blue eyes were bright and avid. "You have been relieved of your vows by the Patriarch of Jerusalem. What were those vows again? Poverty and obedience?"

"And chastity, milady."

Her laughter was low and rich. "Ah, yes. A verbal *ceinture de chastité.*"

His cheeks flushed as he rode with his gray eyes set straight ahead on the twisting limestone road. A silken pompon from a litter cushion touched his hot cheek, then fell away.

"Talk with me, Sir John. My husband gives me all the moody silences I want."

"My speech would bore milady. I only know the art of war and fighting."

"But you know them well. I've heard the manner in which you fought at Shaizar and Aleppo. Of how you and that terrible ball smashed the Saracen charge at Balat. What is it they call it? The whirling devil? One might almost perceive the qualities of a Bohemund or a Godfrey in you. They became kings in Outremer, in these lands beyond the sea."

The languor was gone from her throat, and in its place was a repressed excitement. He caught that note of eagerness and turned to stare down at her curiously. She leaned toward him on an elbow, her eyes flashing.

"A king! King John of Syria! A paladin beyond reproach! A champion of the Cross! A brilliant general! The Saracens know you and fear you. It would not take much to put you on a throne."

"You're mad!" he cried out hoarsely.

"No, not mad. Ambitious. Ah, yes! I'm ambitious as my father was ambitious. But I'm not a man, and I need a man, a strong man, to stand at my side to further that ambition. There's only one man in all the Holy Land who has the sort of strength I need. That man is you, Sir John! You, with a gold crown on your helmet. By the Cross, what a king you could be!"

As if overcome with her own imaginings, the Lady Hodierna fell back into the cushions and lay there, sprawled and relaxed, her body moving rhythmically as it responded to the swaying of the little van. His eyes moved from her lovely oval face down over the tight fittings of her blue silk gown.

John of Lincoln felt his tongue thick and heavy in his mouth. This woman was putting into words the thoughts that had come to him more and more often of late. For where he went in the forefront of the battle, there the gonfanons advanced. The knights and men at arms had come to listen for the scream of his whirling mace, and catch fire from the sound. They looked on him as men once looked on Bohemund the Mighty. And Bohemund was uncrowned king of Antioch when he died.

He shook his head, angry at the weakness in him that would let him listen to this temptress without a challenge. He muttered as if to convince himself, "I'd be a fool to think of it. Besides, I'm a loyal knight. Loyal to my vows. Loyal to my liege lord."

"Yes," she said, unmindful of his words, "it would be very easy to make you king of Outremer. Men have married into royalty before. You could do it, too."

They rode in silence after that, through the stony wastes of the Syrian countryside, where loose gravel lay beside rocks that were streaked whitely with limestone veins, and where the brown hills folded in over themselves to begin the foothills of the Lebanon Mountains, which the paynims called Jebel Libnan.

But now John of Lincoln rode with a fermenting fever boiling in him, and the more he fought the thoughts that swirled in his head, the more they distracted him. To be a king in the Holy Land! To join the kingdoms into a long sword aimed at the Moslem might beyond the Orontes! To wear a crown on his yellow poll, and know his word was law!

It was of this he had dreamed in the English and Norman castles, serving his apprenticeship to knighthood by waiting on tables and furbishing armor. With this in mind he had listened to tales of far travelers in the palace rooms. Too, this hunger had been in him when he set foot on the deck planks of the carrack that brought him to Jerusalem. Scowling in his inner turmoil, he was blind to the fact that the Lady Hodierna was watching him slyly, and that the corners of her red mouth were twisted upward in a contented smile.

Toward sunset they came in sight of the tall stone walls of the Krak. The fortress came upon them suddenly. One moment they were riding the curving road on an upward slope, rounding a ridge of clay and gravel, and the next the Krak of the Knights stood there on its high hill of solid rock. It loomed monstrous in the sunlight, its yellowed stones gleaming as if with gold.

Built with concentric walls that overlapped, it was a magnificent citadel. Its vastness stunned the eyes. On three sides, sheer precipices fell away from under its curtained walls. Only from the east could an entrance be made, by a tower gateway. A ring of outer walls, set with towers, stood around the inner court, which was flanked by even higher walls, where the great strong works and loggia towered upward to overlook the entire bastion.

On the south side, between the inner and outer *enceintes,* stood a moat, filled with water from mountain springs conducted by a stone aqueduct through the southern wall. Sloping talus was set against the base of the high inside walls, encasing the towers with mortar and loose rubble. It was a living mountain of stone, this Krak, gigantic in its sprawling splendor. To the Moslems who eyed it in disgust, it was a fist that held them out of Lebanon, on the hot deserts of outer Syria.

From its chapel tower a sentry could look across the Orontes and see the Moslem town of Homs; north and westward, he saw the Crusader fortress of Safita. Arrow slits that were wide at their stone base and narrow at the top, like hollow stirrups, gave the defenders full vision in which to direct their shafts. Attacking ladders could find no toehold against these sheer escarpments. The Krak was impregnable.

With John of Lincoln pacing his war horse beside the creaking litter, they came up the twisting road on the south and passed by the stone aqueduct. High above, on the warden tower, the red and gold banner of Tripolis flapped in the wind.

A narrow passageway beyond the portcullis and its arched gateway formed the only entrance to the stone Krak. Beyond this gate, an inclined ramp swung sharply left, then cut back to parallel itself at a wide elbow in the sheer walls.

They clattered under the huge portcullis of oak and iron, suspended in grooves in the stone arch by a series of chains and pulleys, and moved slowly up the ramp.

A second gateway beyond the folded passageway gave them ingress into the inner bailey. Here the lower walls of the chapel and refectory were set with delicate arches fitted with stone traceries and Gothic piers.

Esquires in Tripolitan livery came running to take the reins of their horses, while maidservants stared from the outer stairs.

With the lowering sun throwing long black shadows, John of Lincoln escorted the Lady Hodierna into the cool recesses of the great hall. Her hand was warm on his arm as she told him, "I would speak alone with you, Sir John. Later, after we have eaten."

He bowed over her hand, and watched her move away between the battle standards that flanked the long hall, their poles set in iron wall sockets, their gaily colored gonfanons idle in the air. He realized suddenly that he was afraid to be alone with this woman; afraid, and yet curiously eager, for he was remembering vividly the words she had spoken to him on the limestone road that afternoon.

Chapter Two

THERE WERE MANY DUTIES to occupy the attention of John of Lincoln in his first few hours at the Krak. He inspected the huge granaries, and the creaking windmill built atop a tower in the north wall. Under the square openings that flooded the great stable with sunlight he checked stalls and wall rings, and examined the horses tethered there. From the stables he moved on to the armories and forges, and to the sentry walks overlooking every square inch of ground within and outside the massive structure.

As he doffed his suit of chain mail, he held audience with his castellan, an old knight who had fought with Godfrey before the walls of Jerusalem. It was his duty to oversee the defenses of the castle, to check the welfare of its garrison of more than two thousand men at arms. After Basil of Lombardy had gone, the seneschal reported on the grains and vegetables grown in the gardens, and the armorer came to give the numbers and condition of swords and battleaxes, the sheaves of arrows, the bows and mailed suits.

He ate late in the great hall under the groined stone ceiling of the warden tower, on a raised dais covered with rushes. The stone walls were hung with rich arrases, and with wooden shields painted with heraldic devices. A thick tapestry, on which was depicted the death of Roland in the pass at Roncevaux, was draped from chains behind the long table on the dais.

For his relaxation at table, and with the thought of meeting the Lady Hodierna later in the evening, Sir John had put on a short jupe, a jacket of Venetian brocade with loose sleeves. Below the jupe he wore black hose cross-gartered from the knees to the ankles. Around his shoulders hung a chain of gold links, from which was suspended a golden shield enameled with the three corn sheaves of the house of Chester.

He ate a roast mutton that the paynims called kebab, and fresh figs from Egypt, and fine white Syrian bread baked in the brick kilns in the inner court. He drank sparingly of the date wine that a page poured from a silver ewer.

It was over the date wine and goat cheese that a tire-woman found him, with word that the Countess would see him now. He followed the woman up the stone steps of the inner stair and along the wide gallery that flanked the privy chambers, aware that he had been going about his duties at the Krak with a breathlessness that, he had told himself at the time, was only unsureness at new tasks.

His wide mouth curved grimly as he trod at the woman's heels. Unsureness? In John of Lincoln? There was no unsureness in him when it came to war and its varied arts! With his eyes closed he knew the duties of his office.

It was the woman in the chamber beyond the oak door who made him unsure, ill at ease. He was no troubadour to win a woman with song and wit. Rather would he face a score of Seljuks than those blue eyes this night. But her words were still ringing in his ears, as they had rung that afternoon. He walked with temptation in him, but he was a strong man.

John of Lincoln could resist temptation. He told himself that with assurance, as the oak door to the bed-chamber creaked open.

He was not prepared to find the Countess at her bath. The red flames of a burning log in the great arched fireplace were diluted by the pale glow of a score of wax tapers set in bronze floor stands near the tapestried walls.

A standing screen had been set up, and behind it he could hear the splash of water. As he stood there in the doorway, he saw a bare white arm lift above the top of the screen as slim fingers waggled at him.

"Come in, Sir John! I am finding almost as much dust on me as lies between the Krak and the coast."

He did not trust his voice. Although he knew it was occasionally the custom for highborn women to receive visitors at their dressings and undressings, he had never before been in such a position. His heart thudded, and his throat seemed to swell, so that breathing became difficult.

"I could return," he offered, but the rounded white arm waved gaily at him above the screen.

"Why go, messire? I will not be long at this washing. My husband would think it a pleasure to be so received. He would not stand there in the doorway. He would seat himself on a bench and watch me."

There was a bench of red cedar near the fireplace. John

of Lincoln rested himself on its polished top, aware that his legs were trembling. The sound of the dripping water was mightily disturbing to a knight who had lived according to the Templar vows for the past four years.

"I'm almost done," she called to him. "One last soaping, a spray of Arabian perfume . . . There, now."

The Lady Hodierna came out from behind the screen with a towel wrapped about her. Below it, her legs were long and white. She was an exciting vision with her thick brown hair rippling down over her smooth shoulders and back, one white hand clasping the thick woolly material to hold it together.

She went to stand before the red flames of the fire, laughing softly, "The heat dries me much faster than the towel."

Casually she began to move the towel about her body. She twisted to remove drops of water from her legs, and as she leaned forward, the towel gaped. Once again erect, she rubbed the soft fluff here and there, while her blue eyes smiled boldly at him from under the tumbled spill of her hair.

John of Lincoln discovered that his hands were balled into fists against the hunger this woman was kindling in him. They were alone in the large bedchamber, for the tirewoman had gone out and closed the door behind her. The dark shadows of the farther corners seemed to draw in closer about them, sheltering them in mystery and intimacy.

"You summoned me, milady," he reminded her hoarsely.

"To resume our discussion of this afternoon. I said you might be king of Syria, you'll recall? I have been giving thought to it, Sir John."

His laughter was hollow.

She stared at him through the tumble of her long hair where it spilled down over her face. Her red mouth quirked in amusement.

"You do not believe me. You think I talk of miracles. No miracle is needed to put the crown of Jerusalem on your head. Oh, Fulk wears it now, but Fulk is an old man, even if he is married to my sister Melisande. He cannot live long.

"You are a strong man, John. And young! You could unite Acre and Jerusalem, bring peace in place of the eternal squabblings that disrupt Tripolis and Antioch. All Outremer would rise to your banner if you were to lift it against the Saracens, with a claim to the throne."

This was the time to go, but what man could turn his back on such a woman? The thought occurred to Sir John that his confidence in his own strength might be misplaced, but he stood rooted.

"What kind of claim could I make?" he asked.

"A good claim, if you were married."

He brooded at her, knowing that his mind was bedazed by her pallid flesh. He could not think here in this fire-heated room, with this woman exposing herself so wantonly.

John of Lincoln said, "I would need a wife of royal blood. Melisande is married to Fulk. You are married to Raymond of Tripolis. Alice is wedded with Bohemund. Only Yvette remains, and Yvette is but a child."

"I am no child, John of Lincoln," said the Countess, and she let the towel slip. Her laughter was exciting in the shadowy chamber. "You are discovering that for yourself, I see."

She walked toward him, her blue eyes glowing hotly as they sought the fire that lay banked within him. There were the civet perfumes of Arabia in her loose brown hair, and in the creases of her arms.

"I am a woman. Fully a woman, who has borne a child, who knows how to please her liege lord. I would come to a husband experienced and eager to bring him pleasure."

It grew harder for the Crusader to breathe. The fire in the great marble hearth threw red flames upward, but their scorching heat was no warmer than the flesh of this noblewoman who stood so distractingly close.

"You are wedded to Raymond, milady," he whispered.

"And sick of it! He's a mealy-mouth who rants and tirades against me if I so much as laugh. He's jealous of me to the point of madness. He hides himself in his castle of Mount Pilgrim while other men go out to fight his battles."

Her hand rested on the brocaded sleeve of his jupe. Without stirring, she infected him with her own hungers. "Where was he at Montferrand, when his own father was forced to flee the paynims? Only your boldness got Pons safe away to the mountains then. Who smashed the Saracen charge that would have swept away the forces of John

Comnenus on the retreat from Shaizar? Not Raymond! He's no crusading lord like his grandfather, the first Raymond, Count of Toulouse. This Raymond's blood has thinned to water in the Syrian heat. It isn't strong enough to hold the Holy Lands together!"

Lady Hodierna clapped her hands and her tirewoman came and set up her screen before the fireplace. It was fashioned of wood set with copper gilt and glass jewels, and thin silk on which were painted the arms of Toulouse. The silk was thin enough to see through, with the firelight behind it.

The Countess of Tripolis looked at him archly as she went behind the screen. She said, "Have you never dreamed, John of Lincoln? Even in your own cold fashion, has no hunger ever stirred your heart?"

Dreams and hunger! The words were like an ensorcelling wand to brush away the firelight and the painted screen, and replace them with the fens and marshes of his native England. As a boy hunting wild ducks among the reeds, floating through the still waters of the marshes in a flat-bottomed boat, or serving as page to Adelaide, second wife of Henry I of England, he had dreamed of riding a charger through the streets of Jerusalem at the head of a conquering army. Instead of a war horse, he bestrode a wooden bench, and instead of a sword in his hand, he wielded a rag on mail and helms, cleaning armor for the knights.

Aye! He had dreamed in his youth, and he had hungered, too. Hungered for the riches that filled the jeweled coffers of royalty, hungered to own the weapons enhanced by the silversmith's arts, to hold fiefs and lands as did the earls and barons of the court.

He was the youngest son in a family of four boys, in a land where the oldest son inherited everything. It might have been his youthful explorations of the fen country of Lincolnshire or his travelings from London to Normandy with Henry I that gave him the feet of a wanderer. Or it might have been the dreams and the hungers that bedded with him nightly, or walked the palace with him in the day. For five days after Henry knighted him, young Sir John took a big spiked ball at the end of an iron chain, forged for him by a palace armorer, and set foot on a ship of the Five Ports, and sailed for the Holy Land.

His sweat had fallen into the barren sand of Lebanon

and Syria and Palestine for the past six years. Now he was fully grown, in the prime of his manhood, and he owned no more than the black stallion Thane and his weapons, and a reputation as a paladin from Petra north to Tarsus.

Thinking of those dreams and those unfed hungers, he laughed now, and his laughter was edged with bitterness. "Dreams? Hungers? They were my playmates, milady. Dreams I can never make come true, hungers I can never sate!" He went on morosely, scowling at the flames. "Even my dream of helping to free the Holy Lands was an idle one. We own them all. What is left? Fights with paynim bands that come riding into Lebanon like vultures!"

Her laughter was husky from behind the screen. "It seems I've struck flint to hidden steel, messire. For the first time, I find a fire in you."

As if she sought to add fuel to that fire, she released the towel, letting it crumple at her pink toes. He could see her body now as a black shadow on the thin screen, hidden and yet revealed to his probing eyes.

"You add your wealth before it is safe in your castle vaults, messire," she told him. "Imadeddin Zengi is uniting those paynim bands against us. Soon he will have an army ready to attack Antioch. Or if not Antioch, then Tripolis, that he may drive a wedge between the kingdoms. When that time comes, Outremer will need a strong man to lead our banners against the Moslems."

He made a fist out of his big hand, watching her shadow, not knowing whether he balled his fingers against his anger at thought of Imadeddin Zengi or his hunger at sight of the shadowy beauty of the lady of Tripolis. John of Lincoln was aware that he could no more have turned from that shadow screen than he could transform himself into a fish. He watched a shadow nightdress lifted and donned, watched a silhouetted foot step into a shadow slipper, phantom arms lift to tie ribbons on the blackly outlined gown.

He said heavily, "We'll sweep Imadeddin Zengi from our path as Godfrey swept Malik al-Afdhal from the road before Jerusalem."

"Ah, so?" came the throaty voice of the woman. "Like Robert of Normandy, you possess great courage, messire. Yet you lack, as did he, the ability to assess the strategical picture."

The tirewoman took away the screen, folding it, revealing the Countess prepared for bed in her night rail of thin sendal, an almost transparent silk. Her hair was unbound. She was surveying herself in a hand mirror of thin silver. When she turned from the mirror to smile at him, John of Lincoln became aware that her eyelids were blued with kohl, and that her lips were red with salve.

He stood up as she walked to him.

"You are tired, milady. I'll . . ."

"I'm not tired, but—you're afraid. Afraid of your liege lady? In her bedchamber? Sir John, the paladin of the Cross? You who broke the Saracen charge at Balat? Almost you make me feel a gorgon!"

He protested with a thick tongue, and she laughed up at him, warm and near and scented. She captured his hand in hers. "I have not yet spoken my mind to you, Sir John. Perhaps you think me very wanton, to receive you thus so intimately. But there are other intimacies I would as readily grant a man who might aspire to the kingship of Outremer."

She drew him with her to the bed, patting the coverlet.

"I will be frank. Raymond bores me. He will never amount to a mound of copper sols. It would be easy to become a widow, messire. I would not remain long unwedded."

Her hand with the emerald ring on its forefinger gestured at the manner in which the silken gown clung to her, inviting him to give thought to her obvious attractions. "I would bring more than this body to my marriage bed. I would bring the crown of Tripolis, and a fief that stretches from Hama to Beirut."

The fire crackled softly across the room. A shadow stirred where a candle flame flickered against the sudden rush of wind through a narrow spiked window. The blue eyes that looked sideways at him were feverishly bright.

"You understand, messire? There are many poisons to be bought in the *sûk* of the alchemists in Tripolis. Vials of henbane and belladonna, hemlock and certain mushrooms. And there are other poisons that kill without leaving a trace. None would be suspect.

"I would be a widow. You would then be free to wed me, to don the crown of Tripolis. From the throne, with my red and yellow standards and my men at arms, you could hew yourself a kingdom here in Outremer.

"Antioch is weak. Jerusalem is ruled by Melisande, my sister. It would be easy to overthrow them all. Overthrow them, and take command! You bemoan the destiny that refuses you a chance to free the Holy Land from the Saracens? I offer you a bigger fate: Be the man to unite the kingdoms!"

She spoke in whispers, her scented breath at his ear, her hand clasping his arm firmly, hungrily. To the horrified Crusader she seemed a white succubus—one of the alluring female daemons who killed their lovers through the very ardor of their love—flaunting her flesh and her evil schemes for his eyes and ears.

He should rise to his feet and cast her from him. That was his duty, the duty of a Christian knight and a Templar. He had been relieved of his Templar vows, but the greater duty as a knight remained. Like a bell tolling in his brain, an inner voice told him that. His body told him that duty is a harsh and cold thing beside the soft, warm flesh of a woman in the shadows of her bedchamber.

The lady of Tripolis guessed his thoughts, and leaned near. "I called you cold, messire. Can it be that I spoke the truth?"

Her ripe red mouth was inches from his own. Her brown hair spilled over her shoulder until it teased his hand. There was fire in her blue eyes, a fire that leaped out at him.

He tried to speak, but there were no words possible to a mouth that was dry and feverish. John of Lincoln shook his head, as if to make that bell in his mind speak louder. He put his hands out to push the woman away.

Where his palms touched her, he found her skin smooth as satin under the sendal, for she twisted in against him, contriving that his hands touched her body where she willed. The touch of that flesh was too much for a man to fight.

Chapter Three

DAWN CAME UP over the eastern walls to touch the chapel and the inner gatehouse of the Krak with crimson fire. A wind had lifted with the coming of the sun, a hot and searching wind from the distant desert, cousin to the poison wind, the *khamsin* of the Moslems. It stirred the gonfanons on their poles above the ramparts and wafted sand across the limestone road.

John of Lincoln had not slept this night. Toward dawn he had torn himself from the side of the Lady Hodierna, sick and ashamed. He had stamped beneath the stone arches of the gallery that bordered the *grande salle* and mounted the hand-hewn rock steps to the wall walks. For an hour, as the sky grew light, he paced the parapets.

Now he leaned his body against a stone merlon and let the wind soothe his flushed face.

He remembered the confidence with which he had walked into her bedchamber last evening, confidence in his knightly honor and strength of character. Where had it been as he listened to her words and looked at all the bodily treasure she showed him? He chuckled grimly in the dawn. He was not the first man to misjudge his resistance to a woman, but the realization was bitter solace.

His cheeks flushed as he thought of the past night. The sickness and the shame still lay in him, but they were buried now beneath the stirring of a manhood that had long been dormant and forgotten. It was as if John of Lincoln were awakening to life after a long slumber.

She had tempted him with more than her flesh. Her breath had whispered many things to his ears. She offered him the crown of Tripolis, the crowns of Jerusalem and Antioch. Under his banner, the three kingdoms would unite as they had never been united. That honeyed voice commanded him to think of this in terms of a new Crusade. Rivalries and jealousies between Baldwin of Edessa and Godfrey of Bouillon, between Raymond of Toulouse and Bohemund, had resulted in the splitting of the Holy Land between men who forgot the call of Peter the Hermit and remembered only that land and kingdoms could be seized here under the Syrian sun. John of Lincoln could undo that schism if he would.

It was so easy, what the lady of Tripolis had in mind. One death, and a marriage. It could mean much to Christendom. Already Imadeddin Zengi was stirring Islam to a holy war. Soon now the screaming hosts of Mohammed would come surging up from the desert lands, from Damascus and far Baghdad. This time they would be united. There would be no petty jealousies between emir and emir, caliph and caliph, to make the way of the Crusaders easy.

It was against this very attack that John of Lincoln had been sent to the Krak of the Knights, to assume command of its concentric stone walls. But the Krak, and her sister fortress to the north, Safita, were only two stones in the Crusader dam. Why not unite Krak and Safita, Jerusalem and Antioch, to face Imadeddin Zengi with such mailed might that he would be crushed to the very sands over which his Seljuks rode?

But not by murder, not by poison, sapping the life-blood of a man, even such a man as Raymond, he thought bitterly.

The Lady Hodierna had whispered softly in the night, "With all that—me! Hodierna herself as your queen!"

He moved from the battlement down the slab staircase between the chapel and an inner wall, to cross the lower bailey. Temptation was bright before him. A crown, and that white woman!

His hand tightened as if to clasp the black horn handle of his mace-and-chain. The spiked ball was his friend. He knew its every mood and whim; but he did not know the woman who lay in the upper chamber, or the workings of her mind, or how a throne would feel under his rump.

And yet . . . to be king in Jerusalem!

The hot wind fanned his face as he moved across the open bailey that flanked the cloister in the upper ward. Before him stretched the loggia that flanked the arsenal walls.

Something moved in the shadows of the arches, something bent that mewed pitifully as it twisted forward.

When the bundle of rags came into the growing sunlight, John of Lincoln saw a beggar, dirty and unkempt, his shaggy hair blowing in the breeze. Rheumy eyes that were half blind peered up at the big knight. In a hand whose fingers were gnarled and bent, as though from torture, he thrust out a torn felt hat.

"Alms, Lord John! Alms for the praise of Christ!"

The Crusader fumbled at his *amonière serrasinoise,* a little purse of black velvet and silver needlework attached to his copper-bossed girdle. He brought a silver coin out of the alms bag and poised it between forefinger and thumb, smiling grimly. "Men say some of you beggars are holy men, that you have the gift of prophecy, as did the Delphic Sibyl. Do you?"

"Alms, Lord! Alms for the love of the Christus!"

The bony claw trembled as it was stretched out beseech-. ingly. The rheumy eyes glittered for a moment, almost malignantly. And then the hand curved and grasped, and the beggar shrank back into his rags, crooning down at the coin. His head tilted sideways.

"Remember, Lord John—what doth it profit a man? Hee-hee! No profit in the whole world! Only death, and what comes after, hee-hee!"

The beggar went scurrying back into the shadows, and John of Lincoln stared grimly after his flapping rags, with the cackled words ringing in his ears like a sounding tocsin. Aye, what profit is there in the whole world if by winning it a man loses his soul? Or his pride of manhood, without which he is worse than the disease-ridden beggar?

The soft warmth of the *khamsin* was gone, and a chill wind swept down from the mountains to the north. As he felt the wind on him, the big Crusader shivered. He had asked for a prophecy. Had the beggar, like the Delphic Sibyl, spoken in a parable? Was it by chance that the old man had hit upon the one bit of Scripture that might apply to himself?

The shame and the anger in him made him bitter, and the bitterness made him laugh harshly. He was a fool, deluded by the flesh and the whisperings of a woman in the night! The crown was not for him. He was a fighting man, no royal ruler like Henry I of England or Louis the Young in France.

Even within the year, the Lady Hodierna might tire of him and his wars and weapons. She might find another to visit the Street of the Alchemists for her, and one cold dawn John of Lincoln would writhe out his life on the rushes of a bedroom floor,. where Raymond of Tripolis had once writhed and died.

"I'll tell her my mind's made up and have done with this brooding," he growled between his teeth.

He would face her anger and her scorn of him as a man, but he would know himself for no untrue knight. He had taken vows, and been relieved of them; but in his present mood, that seemed only a stronger reason for hewing to them. In the honesty that flooded him, he admitted ruefully that he felt little sorrow. It was not so much the fact that he had lain with the Lady Hodierna this past night as it was the thought that he lacked the power to resist her.

And so, not realizing that it was only the pride of him that had been injured, he came to a stop on the outer stone staircase rising up from the bailey to the warden tower. He drew a deep breath of the early morning air, his eyes closing.

Merely to tell the countess of Tripolis that he had erred was not enough. He must go with her to Tripolis, to confess his sin against Raymond directly to his face, as befitted a guilty knight, and one that sought to make amends as best he might. Offering his body for punishment, he would throw himself on the Count's mercy.

John of Lincoln was aware that there would be no mercy. All the Crusader kingdoms knew the mad jealousy that suffused Raymond II where his countess was concerned. It was rumored that he was more chary of her person than of his crown. Treachery Raymond might forgive; what had happened between John of Lincoln and the Lady Hodierna this past night, never.

He would be taken to the torture dungeons under Mount Pilgrim. He shivered, remembering the tales of tortures that had been garrison gossip from Darum to Saône. His chin lifted and his gray eyes glowed. With something of the martyr spirit buoying his feet, he moved up the open stairway toward the bedchamber he had quitted at the first red rays of the dawn.

He found the Lady Hodierna at breakfast over a wooden table that was set with silver platters of Kafuri plums and dried figs, boiled eggs, and cold milk in a thin glass goblet.

He showed his agitation in the manner of his stride and in the scowl that darkened his tanned face. The vitality of his big body was directed at the woman so fiercely that she paused with a plum midway to her mouth, taking alarm.

"By the holy relics!" she whispered. "Has Raymond come after me? Is he here, outside?"

"He's here only in spirit. I've walked the ramparts in the dawn, thinking about him. About us."

Her relief brought a lazy smile to her mouth. Her body relaxed, and she began eating the plum. He frowned.

"You seem unconcerned, milady."

Her shoulders lifted under the green silk tunic. "There is nothing to concern me, Sir John. I knew what I was doing last night. You have played this Persian game of chess. What I did last night was an opening move in the game we play."

"A game for which I find I have no appetite."

"Naturally." She smiled up at him. "I was aware of that last night. It was necessary to persuade you."

"A persuasion that failed. I leave for Tripolis by noon. I'll be grateful for your company."

She stood at that, and her bosom stirred beneath the green silk bodice of her *bliaud*. "Are you mad? Raymond would suspect the truth!"

His smile was grim. There was a penetential spirit in John of Lincoln at the moment, and in the mood with which penitents offer their backs to the scourge, he rushed on, "There will be need of suspicion, milady. I will tell him everything."

Her mouth opened and closed. She shut her eyes so that her lashes lay like brown fans on her upper cheeks. Then she opened her eyes and glared at him. "Are you mad? Did you meet a froth-mouthed dog on your morning walk? Do you know what such a course will mean?"

"Death for me. Torture, possibly."

"Such torture! You do not know my husband, Sir John! He will have you tied by chains to a metal spit and cooked for days over a fire. In between times, he will have your eyes gouged out, your tongue torn from your throat. I have seen him in the dungeons of Mount Pilgrim, at work on some poor devil of a Moslem he captured."

"No matter. I would rather that than hell-fire."

Her fists beat against his wide chest. "You demented madman! Think of me, and not only of yourself! Do you know what he will do to me?"

"He wouldn't dare harm Baldwin's daughter! At most, he'll put you away in a convent."

"Ah? At most? And can you conceive, in your stupidity, that Hodierna will let herself be shamed before all the world like a harlot from Egypt?"

A finger of sunlight touched her face, revealing the wide eyes and open mouth, the cheeks that were pale in fright as she read the iron determination in this man. Her anger fled from her, left her soft and drooping. Two tears channeled her cheeks as she clasped her hands to him.

"Know pity, milord! Pity for a woman, a mother! Think of my child, my little Raymond!"

She sobbed openly in her seeming abjection, but through the sick misery that her slyly peering eyes detected on the brown features of the big Crusader, she could read his powerful will to do penance. And in that understanding, proud Hodierna of Jerusalem knew towering rage.

She took three steps forward and her open palm cracked hard against his cheek. Once, twice, three times she hit him, with all the strength of her right arm. He stood unmoved, as the Krak would stand against a sandstorm.

"You sniveling clod! You gutless peasant! That I should have chosen a lout like you to sit beside me on the throne of the Crusader kingdoms! That I should have given myself to you in promise! You lack even Raymond's fire. At least, Raymond goes mad when he knows jealousy!"

They stood there facing each other in the stone-walled bedchamber. The woman panted wildly, her cheeks ashen below the pearl caul that bound her rich chestnut hair, the man big and grim, his brows drawn together in a scowl. He told himself, I sound like a monk, prating of hell-fire and damnation. If I were careless of my honor, as so many of the nobles are, I'd laugh at myself. But the shame that lay in him at his betrayal of his knightly vows throbbed like a physical sore.

He said slowly, "Nothing you say can alter my decision, milady. But I want you to know that I blame myself, and not you."

The Lady Hodierna thrust into the opening he gave her. Her hands came out to catch his forearm. Her blue eyes were bright, looking up at him. "You give me hope, Sir John! You mean that you'll go alone to Raymond? Confess your unworthiness to hold office here at the Krak? You'll not mention my name?"

A grim smile came over the Crusader's mouth. "Will Raymond care if I bedded a serving woman? He would laugh at me, and tell me it made a better soldier of me!

Already he thinks me too gloomy, too prone to sit a cutty stool."

"Yes," she murmured as if to herself. "There is only one woman in the Krak he will suspect."

When she saw that her tears and pleas fell on deaf ears, the Lady Hodierna grew cunning. Her hands worked nervously at her girdle of green cloth fringed with gold. Her chin lowered, and she made her full mouth tremulous.

"If only you would give me time. A day or two! A week! I could visit Bishop Gerard and ask his advice. We gain nothing by rushing back to Tripolis now. Just a few days. Is that too much to ask?"

John of Lincoln was an honest man, without guile or cunning. He was a fighting man who wore the red Crusader cross. With that cross he had taken certain vows. He had broken those vows, and being unable to punish himself, sought to do penance otherwise. In his shame and misery, he lacked the insight to see that it was his pride that had been injured: his pride in a will and strength that had played him false.

He said, "By delay, we might find it in ourselves to condone the wrong we did Raymond. I'll take no chance of that. I'm riding in a few hours. Your litter will be ready. Be in it."

He was harsh with her deliberately, knowing that if he stayed longer, she would work the wiles of her womanhood on him, and John of Lincoln was only too keenly aware that he lacked the spiritual stuff to withstand her. The action he contemplated must be undertaken now, or it would never be done.

She nodded her agreement, but in the shadow of her eyelashes her blue eyes glinted. Tripolis was two score miles from this part of Lebanon. It would take a full two days to reach its ravines. In that time, the Lady Hodierna would have many opportunities to snatch back the life she was riding to lose. Under the shelter of her light mantle she put slim fingers on a dagger hilt and closed them until her knuckles gleamed white through the flesh.

Chapter Four

THEY LEFT THE STONE GATEHOUSE of the Krak a little
after noon. John of Lincoln rode in the lead, with the curtained litter creaking behind him. Stretching from the litter to the entry gate were a score of picked men at arms
who wore the red and gold livery of Tripolis. From the
walls, puzzled soldiers and servants peered down at them,
and a few serving maids fluttered silken kerchiefs in farewell. The Crusader never saw them. His gray eyes were
fixed ahead of him at the limestone road that twisted
southwestward to the blue waters of the Buqaia and
Tripolis. It seemed to the woman riding behind him that
he was looking at his death.

It was wild country that the Krak guarded. Nestled
between the Nosairi Mountains to the north and the
Jebel Lebnan to the south, it guarded the narrow passes
of this lonely, desolate land. Sometimes a fox would
bark between a pair of boulders, or a black-maned lion,
lost from its usual haunts in the great Syrian desert,
would roar and cough from the shelter of a thornbush.

Usually when he rode through the lands of the Sepulcher, John of Lincoln was alert to the movement of wings
overhead, or to the sway of an ilex branch that might
signal the passage of a gliding animal. But now his
thoughts were turned inward. He was seeing himself for
the first time in his life, and what he saw he did not like.

For himself to go to Raymond and confess his crime
against him was in accord with knightly teachings. If the
Count saw fit to put him to the rack or chain him over a
slow coal fire, that would be the punishment he merited.
Still, a woman rode behind him, a woman he had ripped
from her bedchamber to meet that punishment with him.
It came to John of Lincoln that he was being unjust to
the Lady Hodierna. He had presumed to judge her. In
his pride he was using the Lady Hodierna as a scapegoat.

A flush sat in his cheeks. Angrily he swung the reins so
that his war horse swerved on the road.

He would send the Lady Hodierna back to the Krak.
Alone, he would ride to Tripolis. He would confess himself to Bishop Gerard, and ask leave of Raymond to re-
tire from command at the Krak, pleading unworthiness.

There would be no mention of the Countess, or of the part she had played in influencing his decision.

They were out of sight of the stone walls of the Krak here, in a little dry wadi that skirted the corner of the Lebanese mountains, but a scant few miles' gallop would bring them within sight of its yellowed walls. When the Lady Hodierna was safe, he would set his face southwest and ride alone to meet his destiny.

He was picturing the woman and her reaction to his change of heart when a faint drumming of hoofbeats sounded in his ears. His yellow head came up, and he turned sideways in the high wooden saddle the better to gauge their direction.

He saw the dust cloud first, dun and misty, rising like the smoke of wormwood fires from the floor of the wadi. Three figures showed black in that haze of dry dust, but even from this distance he knew them for the woman and the two squat warriors he had rescued yesterday—how long ago that seemed!—from the helmeted Seljuks of Imadeddin Zengi.

A larger dust cloud mushroomed behind them to betray the presence of a great number of galloping horses. Sir John waited for no other warning. His golden spurs drove into the black stallion as he catapulted toward the curtained litter.

"Saracens!" he roared, waving a mailed arm at the men who rode behind the Countess. "Forward at the gallop, ten of you. You others, form yourselves about the Lady Hodierna."

With his metal fingers he opened the litter curtains unceremoniously, wincing at the scorn he discerned in her blue eyes. It was on his lips to beg her understanding, to inform her that he had been about to go on alone, without her. But there was no time for that.

"You must descend, milady. Consent to mount a horse. There are Moslem raiders some distance away, and coming fast. I will essay to hold them off. You'll be able to return to the Krak in safety."

Her bosom lifted under the thin silk of her purple and gold *bliaud*. "You poor fool! Once you free me, do you think I'll ever see you alive again?"

Her hand came out from under the woolen mantle that had been thrown across her thighs. In her white fist she held a thin dagger. "Go find the death you seek, messire knight! Or come back to me, and find it waiting for you. I play for high stakes. I'll have no mewling sabbatarian stand in my path!"

His face was hard under his flat helm and its attached camail hood, which he had thrown over his yellow hair. "By your leave, milady! I urge speed."

A black rage shook the Countess. She pursed the red mouth that had been so melting under his kisses, and spat at him. "You'll not escape me, Sir John! I'll be your death. Wager on it!"

And then she was past him, setting a sandaled foot into the stirrup held up by a man at arms, swinging up and sidesaddle on the palfrey that had paced behind the litter.

She paused, framed against the blue sky in her purple *gunna* bordered with gold threadings and girdled with golden plates set with rubies from Mysore. Her contemptuous eyes glinted down at him. "Remember it, messire! Find death here, or by the True Cross I'll send death to find you!"

And then she was off and galloping swiftly, her men at arms wheeling to follow, lifting a golden haze behind their hoofs.

Ten men sat their horses and looked at him. With this half score, he must hold the host that rode beyond those three oncoming figures. A grim smile touched his mouth. The Lady Hodierna had advised him to find death this day. It was wasted advice. Death rode fast to meet him.

As he swung up on the nervous war horse, his right hand lifted the mace-and-chain, gripping it so that it dangled outward at an angle from his thigh. His prick spurs jabbed and the black stallion lunged forward. After him came the men at arms, kite shields slung at their left arms, long swords flashing in the air.

He could see the two little men who flanked the oncoming woman as they turned in their saddles, firing their short bows, sending those black lacquered arrows upward through the dust cloud toward their pursuers. The trousered woman veered toward them, bringing the squat Mongols with her. They met in a welter of dancing horses, with dust sifting down dry throats, excited eyes spreading excitement in their glances.

From behind her black veil the woman said, *"Y'Allah!* Greeting, Lord! We meet again."

She spoke the lingua franca of the Holy Land, but in strange accents that were like some barbaric music. Under her black aba she held the jeweled hilt of a scimitar. On her left hand, with which she gripped the embroidered reins of her big Kashgar stallion, she wore the horn hand shield.

"We will not run when they come at us," said John of Lincoln, wondering at sight of a woman with such armament. "Instead, we'll ride to meet them, to give the Lady Hodierna a chance to reach the Krak."

He fancied that her chin tilted proudly under the mesh veil. "Then we from the Land of the Sun shall not run! Too long have we run already!"

She cried out to the two archers in a guttural language that seemed to rasp her soft throat. The squat bowmen glanced impassively at the big Crusader.

The woman said, "They will stay, but they fight their own way. They do more damage from a distance than with close-in work."

John of Lincoln remembered the line of dead Saracens he had seen sprawled from the limestone road up over the hill of the frankincense tree. He nodded curtly.

"So be it. Ride behind me, woman."

"Shirzade rides behind no man!"

She lifted the horn hand shield and bared her scimitar. He shrugged and touched the stallion under him with a mailed toe.

They moved forward at the gallop, with the Mongol archers flanking them, their bowstrings' twang carrying to the Crusader's ears over the thunder of the hoofbeats. Now he could see into the haze that was approaching, and pick out Saracens in striped jelabs over ring mail. Sunlight lay golden on their round shields, and on the curving lengths of their damascened blades.

Sound rose from the dust in a screech of steel as the two lines came together. Straight swords beat against blades that had been forged at Cairo and Damascus, and the ring of steel on the iron bosses of the shields deafened those who fought.

Over the din, every man could hear the screaming whistle of the big spiked ball. It went into the hook-nosed face of a swart Moslem, then fell between his comrade's shoulder blades. Its spikes dripped redly, and bits of hair and flesh clung to its rounded surface.

John of Lincoln fought always in a little space, for no man would risk being near that great mace when it came whirling back to launch itself forward again in a hurtling rush. His right arm lifted and circled, and the spiked ball dropped and dipped, lifted and battered.

This was the usual raiding force they faced. Two score to sixty Saracens, each with a burning hate for their Frank foes, each with the desire to reach paradise in a battle with the infidels. Their very fury fought for them. They darted in under the sweeping length of the long Crusader swords, and their shorter scimitars thrust upward between chinks in flexible chain mail. But more often than not, that strong mail turned their lighter blades while the straight edges of the Christian weapons sheared through pointed helmets or ripped jagged edges in their mail. Their blades, of laminated steel from the forges of Damascus, were three feet long. Only beside the crushing power of the Crusader swords were they light, but that lightness counted heavily against them in the heat of battle.

Spurring madly, John of Lincoln struck a great wedge in the line of Moslems. The wings of the Saracen line folded in behind the Franks, but none could hold the spiked ball and the men behind it so that they could be surrounded. John of Lincoln drove into the thin line, and when the Moslem wings folded in to encompass him, he turned his black stallion and rode back and through them.

Scimitars glanced off his mail. Some he caught on his triangular shield, with its white field charged with a great red cross. Some his whirling ball broke in its downward crash. His men could not see him, but they could hear that screaming whistle, and it blew courage into their hearts and strengthened them against the shouts and clashing weapons of the Saracens.

The fight drew away from the dry wadi and moved across a sloping hill and onto the dry and barren plain of Jun Akkar. Dead men and wounded men lay side by side behind them. High in the air, as black as their shadows flitting silently across the stony ground, groups of vultures were gathering.

Many times had John of Lincoln fought the warriors of Islam. Usually they joined battle and fought savagely, then raced off to attack again. But these men hung on with the grim tenacity of a Nottingham bulldog. It came to him that the woman at his side, with her horn hand shield and the scimitar that cut and thrust in narrow openings, was the reason for that tenacity.

From the open plain to the rising foothills of the Jebal Lebnan they fought all through that long, hot afternoon. Now there were only three men at arms still beside John of Lincoln. They had fought savagely. They had slain two to their one, and the Lady Hodierna must be safe by now within the sloping walls of the Krak.

With the first dusk of evening, the Moslems drew back to lick their wounds. In the little silence, John of Lincoln heard a bowstring twang; and one of the warriors, who had bent to run his blade into the ground, slid forward, a feathered black shaft protruding from his ribs. Another bow bent and straightened, and a second Musselman crumpled.

He had forgotten the archers. Looking back across the way they had come, he could see men here and there, bent in the stiff awkwardness of death, with those lacquered shafts jutting upward from throats and chests.

"My men are picked for their accuracy, *khawand*," murmured the lady of the veil at his elbow. "They carry spare quivers under their saddlecloths. When the tide of battle passes, they return and take back their shafts. We are far from home in these lands. There are no Mongol fletchers to make them new arrows. They must conserve those they can."

He bowed his head. He was hot and wet inside his mail. The ache of tired muscles, cramping now that the heat and excitement of actual battle were behind them, overcame him with a pall of weariness.

There was bitterness in his chest. He had fought like a Roland this day, seeking the death the Lady Hodierna had prophesied for him. Ironically, the reckless courage with which he went to meet that death so inspired the men who trailed his war horse that together they had shattered the Moslems before their swords.

Across a space of one hundred yards, Saracen and Frank now eyed each other. From somewhere out of sight a bowstring twanged. No man saw the flight of the black arrow in the dusk until one of the Islamic swordsmen went down with buckling knees, feathers jutting from his throat.

A Moslem cried, "*Wallahi!* This is an accursed place! Even the very air sides with the Frangi!"

There were shouts of agreement from his fellows. They mounted and spurred, and they came in one last foray at the standing figures on the little hill. There was no time to seek stirrup and saddle. There was only time to face that charge, those upraised scimitars, those dark faces under the spike-topped helmets with the upcurved noseguards, the foam-flecked lips of trumpeting horses.

The mace-and-chain swung and bashed. The slim scimitar of the lady of the veil slid and thrust. Long Crusader swords hacked. And then the Moslems were gone, careening on past the little mound and riding off into the dusk.

The three men at arms were dead. They had faced the brunt of the attack that swarmed over and around them, leaving Sir John and the woman to one side. They had met the charge and fought it and gone down, and now they left the big Crusader alone with the woman.

Not quite alone. The two squat bowmen came riding up from the flank of the hill, their shaggy ponies fitted with laquered leather reins and saddles, and hide bowcases slung to the left of the saddle and quivers of black-feathered arrows at the right. Their flat faces were shadowed by the wide, upturned fur brims of their conical felt hats. Behind the high cantles of their saddles were slung sheepskin-lined barracans, long pieces of woolen cloth on which they slept; and which, on the flat wastes of their native steppes, served as hood and cloak against the biting winds.

It was the first close look the Crusader had of them. As they reined in, their opaque eyes held steady on the woman. When she spoke to them, they dismounted and went from body to body, removing their shafts. Their ponies followed, heads down, feeding on the stunted grass.

The woman turned to John of Lincoln, and now he could see her dark sloe eyes shining brightly above the torn mesh of her veil. "*Khawand,* never have I seen a man fight as you did this day. Not from far Karakorum, which borders the desert sands of the Gobi, to the Nile of the Fatimids is there such a champion of champions, such a *bagatur.*"

"Nor such a fool," he growled, bending to rub the macehead across the dirt of the hill.

"Allah steals a man's wits sometimes," she admitted.
He glanced up. "You are a Moslem?"

"I am Persian, from Samarkand, to the east, above the
mountains of Ind, along the Oxus. My people are Khorosan nomads, but within the City of the Tall Walls, I am
a princess. I am Shirzade."

He smiled up at her from where he was hunkered
down, brushing the cleansing sand from the steel spikes.
"I am John. Years ago I lived on the east coast of an island
we know as England. My father has four sons. I am the
youngest." He laughed a little, remembering, and his
hands stilled. "It's like being the last beggar in a string of
alms seekers to be the youngest of four sons in a land
where only the eldest inherits the baronial fiefs. A passing monk spoke to me of the Holy Land, and of Tancred
and Bohemund, and of Robert of Normany, who was
a lazy man but a good fighter."

"And so you came across the seas to the land of Outremer to offer your big pointed ball to the Crusader
kings," she said thoughtfully. "John. It is a good name.
We know it as Yukhannan. To me, you shall be Yukhannan."

He stood now, discovering that she came only to the
height of his heart. It was a good height for a woman to
be, he considered, for it made her lift her face to look at
him. He could see through a rent in the black veil, and
what he saw was a wide, curving mouth as red as a Si-
berian ruby, set like a pouting fruit in skin the color of
ivory. Her eyelashes were thick and black like soot,
fringed as an Oriental fan is fringed, veiling black sloe
eyes.

"Shirzade," he said, and felt gratitude to the Lady
Hodierna for awakening the manhood of him that had
slumbered all these years, so that he could look down at
a lovely woman and notice the red ripeness of her mouth
and the mystery of her slanted eyes.

Thought of the Countess of Tripolis brought with it
a numb despair. She had been behind the thick walls of
the Krak for hours now. Perhaps she had dispatched a
fast courier to Raymond at Mount Pilgrim. Or she might
take a larger escort, and ride at once to the coast. In one
way or the other, she would be at Raymond's ear before
two dawns.

He could never go back to the Krak.

He could never ride into Tripolis, or Antioch or Jerusalem.

The Lady Hodierna would see to that; she and her husband would take certain steps, and some dark night or early morn a bit of poison or a knife blade would find him out. It was too late to confess to Raymond. It had been too late when he sent the Lady Hodierna riding back to the fortress. His cheeks flushed at the story she would tell her liege lord.

The veiled woman was watching his face closely. She stirred, and with her stirring a faint fragrance came to the man in mail. She lifted a hand and moved it in an arc. "The stars—which the Mongols say are the fires of their dead—grow brighter by the moment. Night is on us. We have dried goat's flesh, and barley that we will soak in a little wine, and a few dates and apricots."

John of Lincoln had not eaten all that day. He had risen from the bed of the Lady Hodierna and stalked the ramparts, and after that had seen to their journey to Mount Pilgrim. Hunger burst in him now like smoldering wood into flame.

They mounted and rode a little way to a dry water bed. Here the Mongol archers made a small fire of dried dung, and they sat about the flames and ate.

As they chewed on dates and apricots, washing the fruit down with tart wine, John of Lincoln studied the woman covertly. He was discovering that her black veil was a challenge. It masked features he found himself surprisingly eager to unmask, and lent the woman an aura of mystery that she did nothing to dispel.

Since he could not see her face, he looked at her body. She wore tight sheepskin trousers that flared below her knees to expose red leather boots. From her shoulders to her rounded hips she was sheathed in an embroidered *salta,* a short jacket ornate with golden thread. From the manner in which it clung, he judged her waist to be slim and willowy, and her bosom almost generous.

A scarlet velvet turban, draped in tiers, framed the silk gorget to which was attached her black face veil. She ate daintily, never moving the veil so that the Crusader saw more than a disquieting glimpse of her red mouth.

Once she caught his stare, and smiled at him. "In my land, it is the custom to hide the face of a woman from a stranger's regard."

He was aware that the women of Damascus and Baghdad were sequestered in harems. He had ridden into Biza behind the black and white banners of the Templars, and had seen struggling Moslem women dragged from the latticework grilles of the Oriental seraglios. They had not minded when lusting Franks bared their bodies, but they fought like screaming wildcats to protect their faces.

Shirzade sighed heavily, lowering her long-lashed eyes to the fruit in her hand. "I had hoped to find shelter among you Frankish people. But Imadeddin Zengi will not let me get close enough to the Krak to beg sanctuary. He wants me and my archers. So does Unur of Damascus. Tell me, Frank, can I find that sanctuary? Will you speak for me to your people?"

The Crusader chuckled grimly. "At any other time, I'd have said yes gladly. Now I'm an outcast. Yesterday I commanded at the Krak. Today, after a night spent with that woman in the litter—"

His great shoulders shrugged, their mail reflecting the red light from the flames. The woman leaned forward and put a ringed hand on his wrist, as the thin mesh veil quivered to her breathing.

"Tell me, Frangi. It will relieve your mind."

He would never see the Persian again, after this meal. He said to the night around them, "Why not? What have I to hide that the Lady Hodierna won't scream from the ramparts of Mount Pilgrim to the Christian world?"

And so he told her, excusing the woman and blaming himself for the flesh that would not obey the dictates of his will. Of those hot whispers in his ear, offering the crown of the three kingdoms to a strong man, he spoke lightly, disparagingly. He was a little surprised to discover how avid this woman was for his words. She leaned forward, her sloe eyes brilliant above the veil.

"*Inshallah!*" she said when he was done. "As Allah wills it, so a man must play out his destiny. You came across half the world to this barren land. I came as great a distance to speak with you here, before this little dung fire. Who can say you did not do right in taking this Frangi woman? Or in refusing her?"

There was a strong fatalism in this woman of the Khorosan steppes. "It is ordained what we do and where we go. The paths of the men and women that cross our own are laid out for their feet. Many moons ago my father sent me by caravan to Damascus, to wed Shibab ed-Din Mahmoud, who was sultan there. In the long months it took to cross the Oxus and the salt deserts and to pass through Baghdad, Mahmoud was murdered. Unur, his prime minister, elevated his younger brother, Jemal ed-Din Mohammed, to the sultanate. Now, in less than two years, Jemal is dead, and his infant son rules, with Unur as the power on the throne."

She paused, and under the brocaded bodice of her *salta* her bosom lifted proudly. "Unur is an old goat! He received me with fair words and honeyed apologies, and offered me his own hand. *Mashallah!* It was wrinkled and withered and old. I would as soon mate with a mountain ram. So I fled, with ten of my Mogul archers. Unur sent an emir after me with a company of men, and to them I lost five of my bowmen.

"Imadeddin Zengi, who is wed to the Princess Zumur-rud—the infant sultan's grandmother—seeks any excuse to quarrel with Unur, whom he accuses of dealing loosely with him. He too sent men to find me and bring me to him. To those Seljuks I lost three more archers. Now I am left with two. Two bowmen and a woman—against Imadeddin Zengi and Unur of Damascus."

In her anger and her pride, she took to striding back and forth in the firelight. She was barbaric and haughty in her worn garments. Every fold wafted the perfumes of Tibet and Malaya to his nostrils.

"I thought at first that you could help me. My people of the steppes are Nestorian Christians, some of them. They're wild and untamed, and someday they'll sweep west across this land with their ponies and their bows. But now they are far away and I am lonely."

He rose to stand close to her, smiling grimly at the eyes that were misted with nostalgic tears. He said, "Within one day I've failed two women. I can offer you nothing but a weapon."

She shrugged resignedly and stared downward at the flames. From this angle, the rents in the mesh veil gaped wider, and now he saw her fragile nose and the sweep of her mouth and part of a dimpled chin. With an intake of breath, John of Lincoln knew her for the fairest woman between the fens of Lincolnshire and her own Samarkand.

At his gasp she looked up, and the veil fell into place. Her black eyes brooded at him. "You have seen my face. I can read it in your eyes. In my land it would mean your death. Here—"

She sighed with hopelessness and went off a little way by herself. A bowman came and spread a large barracan of black wool, and she lay down on it, drawing a fold of the barracan over her. John of Lincoln regarded her a moment, aware that the Mongol archers were watching him warily.

He moved to his big wooden saddle where it lay on the ground. From the saddlecloths he made a pillow, and, putting his head on it, he settled back to sleep. His last thought before he slumbered was whether the woman and her Mongols would be there when he woke.

An ivory hand with long fingers shook him awake to the red dawn. Shirzade knelt beside him, her clothing freshly brushed. He noted that the rents in her black veil had been repaired sometime between dusk and this early morning.

"We breakfast, Frangi. If you wish, join us."

She turned and walked away, and the sight of her red leather boots moving across the dun sands made the Crusader lift himself from the saddlecloths on which he had slept and stretch in the cool spring air.

Over the last of the dates, the Persian woman asked, "Which way do you ride? By your words, the fortresses and cities of your people are barred to you, except you seek death."

There was bitterness to be discerned in John of Lincoln's voice when he replied. "Imadeddin Zengi and Unur of Damascus will be looking for you. The Lady Hodierna will have her liege lord out hunting for me. Where else should we go but the one place none of them will expect?"

Shirzade paused with a bit of barley bread halfway to her white teeth. Her upraised brows asked a question.

"Damascus," he said. "No Christian knight would seek hospice there, among the paynims. No woman fleeing a grasping prime minister would seek shelter in the city he governs."

Her white hands clapped together as her laughter rose full and strong in the warming air. He liked that laughter, finding it honest and natural, and thinking of that laughter, he thought also of the redness of her full lips.

"Hai! You are a *basheer*, Frangi! A messenger of good news! I knew it when I first saw you riding down the slope of that hill, swinging that great spiked ball. Damascus! I would never have thought of it! Sofodai! Jalagga! Attend me!"

She told the Mongols of his plan, but they only shrugged and grunted. It made no difference to them where they fought and died.

They saddled and mounted and moved forward over the foothills of the Lebanon mountains. John of Lincoln took the lead, his eyes searching the ground for the rockiest stretches, that their mounts' hoofs would leave no trail.

As he rode, he waved his arm at the towering hills around them, shot through with whitish limestone, covered with stands of stone pine and locust trees. Higher up were dwarf oak and ilex thickets, and scattered thorn shrubs. It was a desolate land, but the deep gorges and precipitous canyons afforded fine shelter for a small party.

"We can follow the valley between the mountains as far southward as Galilee. Turning east, we'll come down to Damascus without ever setting our horses on level ground."

It was a good plan, and the Crusader knew it. But he would have been less than human if he had not responded when the woman turned her eyes on him in admiration. He drew a deep breath of the cold air, and felt it tingle along his veins. Her hand reached across to him as they sat their horses side by side, and pressed his arm hard.

"It is the will of Allah that we met, Yukhannan. The Prophet guided your steps. He whispered in your ear as you lay with that Frankish woman. He opened your eyes. He brought you to me."

The Crusader grinned. "Not Allah, but the Christus."

She laughed with him, the wind stirring her blood as it did her gray wool aba. She knew that this big Frank found her good to look upon. For the first time in her life, Shirzade, a Khorosan princess from the steppe world of distant Samarkand, felt the urge to loosen her veil to a man.

Her laughter stirred a chemical change in the blood of the Crusader. His face, more used to grimness than mirth, relaxed in a grin. When she challenged him to race her to a distant line of thorn thickets, he toed his war horse forward with a shout.

Behind them the Mongols glanced at each other with their opaque eyes. Then they tucked their chins into the fur collars of their woolen cloaks and galloped their shaggy ponies where the others led.

Chapter Five

IMADEDDIN ZENGI brooded in his round, wide tent of striped Cathayan silk. He was a short, stocky man in early middle age, his dark hawk features given added dignity by a short, pointed beard. He wore a loose silken caftan, in which he took his ease against the time when he must don the shirt and chain mail that hung now, with his steel scimitar and round shield, on the central tent pole. At his elbow, on a low table set with kufic inscriptions in lapis lazuli around its border, were glasses of cool sherbets and silver platters of Asini grapes and Tamri figs.

Imadeddin Zengi was a man used to war. He had been champion of the Abbasid Caliph, and under his banners had broken the Baghdad might at Wasid. For that conquest the Caliph had named him Atabeg of Mosul.

Since he was a man who conceived himself as blessed by Allah, he urged a holy war against the Franks, with the lands of Mohammed the Prophet as their goal. He took Aleppo in the name of his master, as an example to the emirs of the Moslems. But when Imadeddin Zengi could accomplish his ends by suave tongue and rich gifts, he saw no need to fight. He counseled unity between the emirs, pointing out that the Frangi were their common enemies. Personal differences between the Seljuk Turks, which had made them as water against the inroads of the first Crusaders, should now be forgotten.

He was well along on his chosen path. Shaizar and Homs, Montferrand and Hama were allying themselves with his banner. But jealousies and old grievances were enemies that accepted no flattery or gifts. Almost despairing of binding the Saracen cities together, he found himself turning his eyes eastward for other allies.

His first attempt in that direction had been greeted by failure. And so, as he sat at his ease in his domed tent, Imadeddin Zengi was perturbed.

His dark eyes coldly regarded the three mailed captains who stood so sheepishly before him. Their spiked helmets and upcurving noseguards, their collars of Damascus chain mail and striped jelabs proclaimed them men of importance. Expensive boots of Persian leather held the woolen trousers that had been tucked into them.

"A woman," he said softly. "A woman from Samarkand with two archers and one Frangi knight! Yet they slip from your hands as water would slip through my open fingers."

His palm hit the inlaid tabletop and made the goblet of Raiy glassware topple. Imadeddin Zengi sat up straighter as the fine glass shattered near his brocaded felt slippers.

"You call yourselves soldiers of Allah? You're not fit to be pigs rooting in the gutters of Aleppo for a meal!" He saw his captains straighten as anger smoldered in their bright, dark eyes. "I said pigs! Pigs depend on their own wits for survival. You attach yourselves to my generosity, but do you concern yourselves to earn its fruits?"

One of the captains, a slim man with a crescent scar across the brown skin of his right cheek, lifted his aristocratic face proudly. "It was no ordinary Frangi. It was the whirling devil!"

Imadeddin Zengi grunted. He had seen this whirling devil fight at Baza'a and at Montferrand. "You had sixty men. Sixty men! Were they timid women I gave you? Singing girls? Bayaderes?"

The tall captain flushed until his scar was hidden by the rush of hot blood to his face. "They had little archers, men who shot small bows from horseback. And twenty Frankish men at arms. We slew the Christians. All but the whirling devil."

"And the Persian woman escaped! Now only the Prophet knows where she is!"

The Atabeg of Mosul bit his full lower lip. He would have given much to put his hand on the Khorosan beauty, if only for the fact that Unur of Damascus wanted her for his own. But there was more than petty spite in this man. He was a visionary. He was seeing beyond Damascus, and even beyond Baghdad on the muddy Tigris. He was looking eastward to the great plains beyond Raiy and the salt desert, to the Oxus and the steppes beyond that river, where bands of nomad warriors who fought from horseback with short bows and black arrows lived in black felt yurts. Those Mongol nomads ranged from Samarkand to Kasghar, and on to far Karakorum, the city of the black sands. They were as many as the dates on the trees of Syria. It was to those hordes that he looked for allies against these troublesome Crusaders.

Imadeddin Zengi knew that he could unite those hordes with his Seljuk Turks by a marriage of his son Nureddin to this Persian beauty. Almost, she had been within his reach. Now he had lost her, and the thought that he might also lose those hordes of mounted bowmen as allies maddened him.

He stood erect and his proud eyes flashed with fury. His three captains fell back before that rage. He spoke to the scarred aristocrat, and his voice was level with a deadly grimness.

"Nasran ibn-Afdal, you will take five score mounted swordsmen and five score mounted archers. You will ride south and west to Homs, which looks across the Orontes at Krak. You will proceed with caution there, through the passes into the Frangi lands. You will learn where this Princess Shirzade has gone. You will go after her and bring her back to me. On your head is your failure!"

The captain gasped in his throat. One hundred wielders of the scimitar! One hundred archers! It was a striking force that made the eyes glisten.

As if catching his thought, Imadeddin Zengi came close to him, peering intently into his fine dark eyes. "I give you that many men so there will be no excuses, Nasran ibn-Afdal! Are we bayaderes that we let one Crusader rout our True Believers?"

His captains salaamed and bowed out of the great coned tent. Imadeddin Zengi hit the tent pole with a hard, callused palm. To ally himself with those uncounted bowmen of middle Asia, he would take the saddle himself, if need be! There must be no failure.

In the privy chamber of the great castle of Mount Pilgrim, which looked out over the sea walls of Tripolis, the Lady Hodierna was closeted with her liege lord, Raymond. Below them, the kitchen kilns were roaring with freshly laid fires, and the smell of roasting lamb and wild duck stole up through the galleries and the privy stair to their bedchamber.

Raymond did not heed the sounds of his castle nor the rich scent of the food he would soon be eating. His attention was fixed on his young wife, who stood in a silk chemise before she resumed her dressing.

"You did well to send a messenger to me, Hodierna," he assured her as she tilted a silver mirror to gaze at her lovely face, "so that I could send men at arms to escort you back here at once. It was foolish to leave Mount Pilgrim in the first place."

She brought her blue eyes to him. "You promised I should have a holiday. I had never seen the Krak. If you hadn't sent that ape along to guide me, all would have been well. Guide! It was more than guide me he wanted to do!"

From the corner of her eyes she saw his fist clench at the quick, hot rage that beat in his veins. The Lady Hodierna knew the temper of her liege lord, and, gauging it, could feed it as she willed.

He said now, "Your very anger against him leaves me suspicious. I know Sir John of Lincoln. He was a Templar. He would not soon easily forget his vows."

"Vows from which the Patriarch of Jerusalem relieved him before he took the road to Krak."

He scowled at her. "That was your doing! It's been in my mind to turn the Krak over to the Templars or the Knights Hospitalers, for it's devilish expensive to maintain. But that time is not yet come. And a Templar may not hold its commanding office while still acknowledging the sovereignty of his order, as you yourself so astutely pointed out."

Carelessly Hodierna pushed down the sleeve of her thin garment until her shoulder gleamed in the candlelight. His eyes fastened on that white skin, watched as her fingertips caressed her flesh.

She said dreamily, "He came to my bed while I slept and took off my night rail before I could prevent him!"

Count Raymond breathed harshly. His balled fist hit the edge of a bedpost. "Enough, enough! Even if I believed you, there's no need for details!"

Her eyes clouded. "Even if you believed me?"

"Ah, Hodierna! I'm your husband. I see how your eyes move from man to man, as if measuring them. Your honeyed words belie the gleam the sight of those men bring to the eyes I love!"

She shrugged the sleeve of her silken shift back into place. Petulantly she raised the mirror and resumed her preoccupied admiration of herself in its hard polished surface. With the tip of her little finger she smoothed the perfect arch of her brow, casually, as though he were not there.

He came closer. Now he grew aware of the civet perfume nestling in the folds of her undergarment. His dark eyes began to glow.

He said between tight lips, "I'd sooner believe from your attitude that when you attempted to seduce him to to your bed, he refused you. It would the more accord with your anger."

Hodierna smiled and hummed.

Count Raymond went on, "If he'd done the things of which you accuse him, you'd have welcomed him with open arms!" The lord of Tripolis knew his wife.

That Hodierna also knew her husband was evidenced by the fury with which she whirled on him. The silver mirror clattered to the floor. Her white hands lifted to the lace border of her shift. With one savage tug, she ripped the thin stuff from her shoulders.

"Look now on me," she sneered. "See me as he saw me!"

He cried out harshly. His hand came up, and for an instant Hodierna thought he meant to strike her. Then he sobbed in his jealous passion, and his hand fell.

She looked straight at him, and now she made her voice soft and soothing. "I fought him, Raymond. Despite what you call my roving eyes, my body has known only yours."

Hodierna kissed her husband there in the little chamber and so contrived herself that he whispered into her ear, "It shall be done as you wish. Everything you want, I'll set myself to accomplish!"

"A man from Alamut, a member of the Assassin sect," she breathed. "A man who serves the Old Man of the Mountains. An Ismailite who will go to the ends of the earth to kill the man who is pointed out to him!"

She ran her lips across Raymond's cheek to his mouth, and clung to him. His strong hands held her, and she could feel him nod agreement, even as his senses swam.

As he watched her don a surcoat of rich brocade and drape her brown hair in a golden caul, over which she hung a wimple of yellow silk, Raymond realized that he was a weak man where this woman was concerned. But when she turned her face to him and smiled promisingly, the little quirk of conscience that ran in him was deadened. It was enough that she was with him, and smiling tenderly.

Raymond of Tripolis ate little in the great hall below his bedchamber that evening. He toyed with a silver goblet that was only half full of dark red wine, and his eyes brooded out over the long tables set before his dais.

His captains and some of the richer merchants from the famed underground bazaars sat side by elbow with learned savants from the medical school of Tripolis. Their conversations made only a low murmur in his ears. Even when the jongleurs came and sang, and the dancing girls of the Moslem quarter gyrated and twisted in the open space between the tables, he gave them little attention.

For his somber eyes were fastened always to the door that led from the great hall to the forebuilding. When his castellan came out of the shadows and made a motion at him, he sat up straighter, and reached across to put his hand on the arm of Lady Hodierna.

"The time has come," he whispered, and his wife, nodding, gathered a long woolen mantle about her and rose.

They found the Assassin in the shadowy gallery, beside the bulky figure of the castellan. He was a lean man with a dark face whose pointed beard caught at the torchlight from under the draped folds of his hood. He wore a caftan of black wool marked with thin red stripes. To the Count, he seemed a living representation of the Satan he had seen on illuminated church parchments; almost unconsciously he caught himself staring at the shadowed hood for the points that would be his horns. Raymond explained his need. "A big man, this John of Lincoln. He is a Crusader whom the Musselmen call *dair azazil,* the whirling devil. He wears golden spurs to match the color of his hair, and his eyes are as gray as the lead that comes from Karman."

Ahmed the Assassin nodded dourly. It was three months since he had been carried, drugged, into the walled gardens of Alamut to taste the rich fruits from Syria and Palestine. There had been a willowy houri who had been as warm as the sultry desert air and as ardent as a penitent slave in the fulfillment of her duties. She had whetted his appetite for another such visit.

All assassins were fed the drug called hashish before they were carried into that garden. Awake then, and possessed of all their senses, they were expected to believe that they had been transported into the paradise of Allah. It gave them pleasant memories and dulled their fear of death, for on a mission for the Old Man of the Mountain, or for whom the Old Man called friend at that moment, they believed they would go straight to that same paradise if they met death on their mission.

It was a pleasant conceit, but one that Ahmed did not believe in. Still, Ahmed was a wise man, and he kept a silent tongue in his head. He had been picked for many tasks such as the one the Lord of Tripolis now gave him.

Count Raymond dropped a velvet purse, fat with golden miskals, into the brown hands of the Assassin. "There is gold there. More will be forthcoming when you return with proof that John of Lincoln is dead."

Ahmed allowed himself the luxury of a rare smile. "The hand of the Assassin never fails, *yah khwaja.*"

It was no more than truth the man spoke, yet Raymond could not repress the shudder that ran through him. Fortunately, the followers of Hasan ibn-al-Sabbah lived cheek by jowl in distrustful friendship with the Franks. Raymond had availed himself of their gifted services more than once in the past. He paid good gold, and he got the worth of that gold in dead men.

For all his protested friendship with the cult of killers, Raymond of Tripolis was never at ease in their presence. Something of this Ahmed suspected, for he showed white teeth between his ruddy lips in a mirthless grin, and his brows drew together thoughtfully.

"The whirling devil may take some finding. I will trail him beyond the rim of the world if I must, but this gold may only be enough to pay my traveling expenses."

The Lady Hodierna fumbled at the forefinger of her right hand, withdrawing her emerald ring. She thrust it at the Assassin, whose eyes gleamed momentarily at sight of that green fire. He masked his greed under drooping eyelids and nodded his head, his lean fingers closing over the jewel.

"*Inshallah!*" he whispered in the darkness, bowing.

A moment later he was gone, his feet leaving no sound on the stone floor of the gallery.

Raymond shivered, staring after him. The warm little hand of his wife recalled his thoughts. She murmured, "My liege lord trembles from the cold of the gallery. It is my duty to warm his blood."

Again Count Raymond trembled, but this time it was because his eyes were fascinated by the warm, lazy smile on the full red lips of this woman at his side. She put an arm about his waist and led him toward the privy stairs that spiraled upward to their bedchamber.

Unur the Aged had served the war lords of his people for more years than he cared to count. Now he was grown old and tired of the cone tents of the battle camps. He found himself directing his thoughts more and more to the softness of woman flesh, and to the intoxications of the scents the slave girls wore. He had fought a great many battles in his time, from the Tigris to the sea. He had warred with Imadeddin Zengi and with Bahram Shah. Twice he had hurled back the Seljuks of Mosul from the walls of Damascus and twice he had taken the field against their atabeg.

It was time now for an old war horse to rest, and to let the younger and the stronger men ride out to do battle. Humoring himself in this conceit, he felt that he was deserving of the same treatment that considerate warriors gave their finest horses. As he sprawled lazily on the piled cushions of his palace seraglio, he nudged the bare neck of a Danishmend slave girl.

"Eh, Ilika? What is it that they do to retired horses? Horses of good stock?"

The slave girl giggled and leaned above him so that her red tresses could tickle his cheeks. "They put them out to pasture, O Master. To pasture, and to—stud!"

She laughed shrilly and collapsed across his chest. He roared gustily and his hands sought her ribs to tickle them in turn. Like children, they caromed off the cushions and rolled across the mosaic tile flooring.

He cackled loudly, grasping her wrists and holding them. "A good answer, by the Prophet! For that I'm going to reward you!"

His hand snatched a curved *kumia* from its scabbard. He threw the jeweled dagger across the cushioned room so that it hit a great copper gong hung on trivets. The resultant clangor filled the chamber with a throbbing ring. Before the sound faded out, he whispered into the girl's throat, "I'm going to give you to Ramid, Ilika. To Ramid of the wandering eyes. You've been coveting him a long time, haven't you?"

Unur shrilled his laughter at her denials. He waved a big, wrinkled hand at her.

"None of your lies, *bint*. I've watched the two of you! I may be old, but I can still see people for what they are. That's how I've come to power! Be quiet, now. You've been a good girl, and it's time for a change of masters. But I'll make Ramid earn you, O Giver of Delights."

Ilika pouted. "You have your eyes on another girl. That's why you want to be rid of me."

A gnarled forefinger dug into her brown flesh. "Eh, eh? And why not? Some days I eat Malban figs from Baalbek, some days I favor Cydonian apples!"

A eunuch in striped silk trousers came to bow before the Mameluke. The old man reclined on an elbow and waved a hand. "Summon the emir Ramid ibn-Ghazi to me. Tell him I've a present for him. A present he'll appreciate."

As the eunuch turned to go, Unur drew the giggling Ilika in against him. Into her ear he whispered, "Serve me with Ramid as you've served me on these cushions, and it may be that I'll set you free, one of these days. Keep him well disposed to my favor, girl."

Ilika assured the Prime Minister that he would be in her thoughts waking and sleeping. His wise old eyes watched her as the hunting falcon watches its prey. He grunted and got to his feet.

"He'll be here within a matter of minutes," he told her. "Go get the anklets I gave you, and the bracelets with the Bahrian pearls set in them. Let Ramid see that you do not come to him as naked as you came to me."

Unur turned his back and went to stand at an arabesqued window that looked out over the great orchards southeast of the city. Behind his back his hands curled and uncurled, as he directed his thoughts to the ivory loveliness of Shirzade, the Khorosan princess from Samarkand, who had been here in Damascus less than a month ago. *Yah!* She had been a temptation even to such an old one as himself, with her sooty lashes veiling those slant eyes, and the black hair piled on her head like jewels in a Sultan's coffers. He had been a fool to let her slip out the Desert Gate.

Instead of trying to woo her with honeyed promises and warm glances, he should have used a fist. *Y'Allah!* That was the way to tame a proud woman! Unur had

seen more than one haughty *sitt* come around to his way
of thinking after a few buffets. He lifted his big fist,
which was wrinkled now, and brown, but still could grip
a scimitar with a strength that drew its source from a
warrior's pride. He shook it in the air, cackling a little.

"*Yah!* My knuckles, until she learns to obey! The fist,
instead of jewels and soft words!"

Eh, well! Unur had made mistakes before, and had rec-
tified them. It was not too late. The Khorosan was running free, like a startled doe before the hunters, somewhere between Damascus and Aleppo. He would have
her found and brought back to him. This time he would
not be so gentle.

He was chuckling over her imagined responses to that
fist when a jangle of golden *khalkhals* announced that
Ilika had returned. On her heels came a slim young emir
in a gaily colored satin caftan, sashed with a wide band of
gold brocade. Pearls were fitted to his small ear lobes.
Below the thin, curving black mustache he affected, his
teeth showed white and even.

Ilika watched Ramid ibn-Ghazi from under her long
lashes. She giggled as his eyes moved up and down, from
her heavy gold anklets to the transparent silk trousers
that were like webbed mist on her legs. He was a devil,
this debonair nobleman! But the bayaderes whispered
that he was more than generous to a girl that pleased
him. It took no bearded *kadi* to tell little Ilika that she
was the cause of the glow in the emir's eyes.

Unur was a wise man. He kept his back turned and
his eyes fixed on the distant orchards. It was not by
chance that Ilika and Ramid ibn-Ghazi found the opportunity to measure each other fully.

When he considered that the young emir had had time
in which to appreciate the generosity of his prime minister, the old Mameluke turned.

He waved a hand at the giggling Ilika. "She is yours,
Ramid. My gift to you, together with the golden *khalkhals* on her soft wrists and delicate ankles. As you can
judge, I have forgotten your failure to catch the Princess
Shirzade and her Mongol archers, when you chased them
out the Desert Gate."

Ramid ibn-Ghazi bowed low. *Hai!* He had seen this
little redhead glide here and there through the seraglios
of his dreams. Now she would glide no more only in his

slumbers. She was his! As he lifted his head, he allowed his fiery eyes to dwell on his most recent possession.

Unur watched him, smiling. As he had told the slave girl, he knew men and the desires that govern their actions. He said now, almost irrelevantly, "The Princess Shirzade thought me too old a coat to wear on her young shoulders when she was last in Damascus. She was to have wed Shibab ed-Din Mahmoud." The old Mameluke sighed. "Unfortunately, he was killed before that happy event. Then his brother died. Now only a child sits on the throne. And Shirzade would not settle for me as a substitute husband. Eh, eh! I was foolish, too. I should have handled her as I would handle a wild mare. Well, no matter!"

The pause as the Prime Minister ceased speaking became uncomfortable. Unur sighed heavily.

Ramid ibn-Ghazi frowned. He said, "I can offer you a blonde Frangi woman I captured on my last raid into Galilee."

Unur waved his hand as if the thought nauseated him. In mid-gesture, he said, "However, if Allah should will it that the Khorosan princess be found, I would not prove ungenerous to him who brought her to me."

The old Mameluke fixed his eyes on the emir, and Ramid ibn-Ghazi stiffened. "It would be an honor, Lord of Generous Givers! Allow me a thousand swordsmen, and I ride at once."

Unur watched them go until the slave girl's golden anklets clanked out of hearing. Then he went back to his thoughts of the Khorosan princess, and the methods he would use to break her spirit.

Chapter Six

THE NORTHERN END of the mountains of Lebanon are formed of deep canyons and gorges. Here nature has scarred the earth with pitted slashes and frighteningly sheer precipices. Snow lies on rock and shale almost to a depth of two feet, even in the springtime of the year.

The four riders who moved southward between these gorges and across their natural bridges of rock drew their woolen abas closer around them and sank chins deep into the fur collars of thick gray barracans. Where the wind went, it drew chilly fingers across faces and hands, and sought out flesh bared by flapping cloth.

From the plains of Jun Akkar southward for all of that first day, John of Lincoln and Shirzade rode swiftly, followed by the Mongol archers. They galloped where they found level stretches of the hard, stone-strewn ground, then walked their mounts over mounds of tumbled talus, or led them afoot up sloping ridges.

At night they made camp on a table rock between towering black crags, where the red glow of the fire drew their open palms above its flames. Nothing binds travelers together more than a sense of danger shared among them, and for the first time John of Lincoln found the impassive Mongol archers grinning at him shyly. The opacity of their black eyes was gone in a trust that made them come bright and laughing as they offered him a bowl of stew they made from three snow hares their black shafts had felled an hour before sundown.

When they discovered his interest in their arrows, they brought a lacquered hide quiver to him, and with the lady Shirzade translating their guttural barks into the lingua franca, they informed him that the greenish-black feathers on the shafts came from the snakebird.

"The snakebird lives on the rim lands around Cathay, and south of the Roof of the World," said the trousered Persian. "It flies from Borneo to Malaya, and on to Ceylon. Its long tail feathers make good fletchings for the Mongol shafts."

John of Lincoln found that the lady of the veil was less distant, too. Her eyes lingered on him more than once over the steaming broth and the bits of barley cakes that the archer called Sofodai had made from a handful of flour from his saddlebag and a cup of melted snow. He fancied that her red mouth smiled gently at him from its silken covering.

And later, with her red leather boots and his mailed feet stretched to the popping thornbrush branches, she told him a little of the world she knew, of fabled Samarkand of the Towering Walls and its golden images of Buddha, of the royal gardens set about with orange trees and tall palms, with waters splashing in the rounded fountains, the *cliwans* tiled and gilded. She held him with a description of the mosques and minarets where the call to prayer rang nightly.

She said wistfully, "I knew I would never see its high walls again, or the fruits that sway in the breeze from the Oxus, when I kissed my father farewell. Still, it was not like this that I pictured my plight. I was to rule as queen of Damascus. Now a child sits on its throne, and a human goat on its palace cushions."

It came to John of Lincoln, there in the cold mountain night, with the wind off the Lebanon peaks whipping down into its deep gorges, moaning and wailing like a demoniac *ghil* of Arabic legend, that sometimes a man was granted a vision of his future. Her words had given him a glimpse of wide brown steppes and of the nomad people who lived on them in their black felt tents. He was discovering a hunger in him to ride across those wide plains and see the frozen tundras to the north, and the unknown, ancient ruins that dotted its flat surface.

"Why not?" he asked the howling wind. Where else was there room for a man who was an outcast from his own kind to ride his horse? None knew John of Lincoln —who would be only Yukhannan of the far lands—on those steppes. Something of the ancient wanderlust that lived a little in all men was born to him in that moment.

He said again, "Why not? We are two displaced persons, you and I. I'm at home on the Lincolnshire fens, while you belong on the steppes of Transoxiana. I'll never see my home again, but there's no reason why you shouldn't go back. You'll be welcome to Samarkand, as their princess. You might even find a place for me in the palace guard."

Slim ivory fingers smoothed the black sable fur on the split of her *tschim* at a rounded knee. "Have you any idea how far it is to Samarkand? Over two thousand miles —with half the world against me!"

"All the world," he corrected glumly, "as long as you're with me. I'm wanted by the Christians."

"Hai! Is this my paladin talking? All the world against us two? Good odds, Frank!"

He caught the momentary flare of savagery in her black sloe eyes as Shirzade felt the blood of nomad ancestors stirring in her body. She made a small fist of her hand and thumped it on her thigh. "If only I had a *tuman* of Mongol archers! Hai! I'd ride up and down this land and take and burn their cities! I'd teach them to hunt a Khorosan princess from the Kara-Khitai like a helpless, wounded bird!"

She paused and sobbed, and her turbaned head fell forward to rest on a bent knee. The wind stirred her neck-cloth, and where it lifted, the Crusader saw thick black hair, glossy and perfumed, against her slim neck.

He growled, "Aye! And I'd ride with you! But to get those archers we have to go across half the earth." He was gruff, wanting to reach out to console her, but feeling awkward and embarrassed at the emotion in him. He laughed harshly. "It will be a good race, we two against the world, in a two-thousand-mile run!"

She shook her head, and he could read the utter weariness in her black eyes. "I'm tired of running. I've fought too many times with my scimitar and hand shield since fleeing the Desert Gate of Damascus. I have no heart for that awful journey back to Samarkand."

He would not let her admit defeat. He stood up and he laughed at her. "I will do your fighting, Shirzade! My spiked ball and my sword will stand between you and your enemies."

"One man? Even such a *bagatur* as you? Ah, no, Yukhannan. It's only a noble dream." She rose. "Better to die here in this alien land. Better to die in slumber."

He put a hand on her arm, and through the wool of her mantle he could feel the softness of her flesh. That touch put a fire in him for this woman, a fire that burned and ate at him as if transforming him into molten metal. He said softly, knowing that his eyes hungered at her, "You'll think differently in the dawn. Sleep and dream of those orange trees. Then come to me and tell me you don't care if you ever see your home again."

John of Lincoln watched her walk away, head down. Sighing, he lay beside the fire, staring upward at the dark blue sky. The stars winked at him, stars that gleamed over English manor castles and over the steppes of middle Asia. He wondered whether they were as clear in the sky from the flower gardens of Samarkand.

It was the Persian woman who waked him once again to the frosty cold of dawn. She knelt by him, and her black eyes glittered in her ivory face.

"Are you a shaman to know the future, Yukhannan? Last night you told me I would dream of Samarkand. I did! I dreamed its fountains sang a song, and its orange trees echoed that song in the swaying of their branches. They sang a song of a paladin from the west." She sat back on her heels, and the trimmed black brows over her eyes drew together. "The fountain waters and the trees sang that I was coming, and with me came a man who would restore Samarkand to all its olden glory, as when the Samanids ruled."

John of Lincoln drew cold mountain air into his lungs. Like wine it bubbled, warming him. He laughed. "We are always weakest before sleep, milady, and strongest in the morning, after rest."

His eyes held hers boldly, and a faint flush, like the tints of the rose sherbet that the Saracens ate, touched the pale ivory of her face above her yashmak. She held her black eyes steady on his as she said, "We must fight only at dawn, then, Yukhannan. For it will need a very strong man to travel the far leagues between here and the foothills of the Hindu Kush."

He stood up and brought her with him, so that the lengths of their bodies almost touched. That nearness gave him the boldness to say, "I will be strong, Shirzade— for you."

She placed her warm palm against his brown cheek. "Aie! You will be my paladin, Yukhannan!" she whispered, and it seemed to the big Crusader that her veil fluttered a little, as if she breathed faster to certain secret thoughts.

They rode all that day between the towering peaks of the Jebel Libnan, cantering steadily southward. The deep browns and yellows of the towering mountainsides were relieved by little green patches of alpine grass and Oriental oak trees. In the distance the towering elevations of the Wadi en-Nusur were broken into tiered terraces of stone, beyond which the travelers could glimpse the blue waters of the lake Yammuna.

Now the heights were leveling. The canyons and gorges of the north yielded to sloping hillsides and stretches of green grassland. To one side the Sunnin thrust snowy tips against the clouds. Below the gravelly ridge they galloped was a valley ten miles wide, split by the southward-flowing Litany.

This was a wild and empty land, for only a few hardy shepherds grazed their flocks on its arid acres. High overhead an eagle circled on widespread golden wings. Brown rock and gray boulders, with an occasional mountain stream flashing silver in the sunlight and stone ledges falling sheer to dizzying drops, were the only things at home in this mountain wilderness.

They came down into the valley by a twisting path that had been old when Ur was young. Mincing hoofs sent little pebbles bouncing and leaping ahead of them. John of Lincoln rode point, his bulk and his black war horse a comforting shield to the willowy Persian, who swayed her bay gelding with the black mane in his tracks.

With grass under their hoofs, the horses rode with higher heads. The smell of water was in their nostrils, and the cold wind off the heights was here a warming breeze.

John of Lincoln reined in, pointing upward at the gorge through the Jebel Keniseh. "We take that courier route over the mountains. Few travelers come this way. Only messengers riding fast with important state documents."

Shirzade shaded her eyes. "Damascus lies beyond it?"

"On the other side of the Jebel Keniseh."

Behind them, from the great plain of Jun Akkar, which lay north of the Lebanons, to this point opposite Beirut, they had traveled seventy miles. They had another few leagues before them, over the pass of the Jebel Keniseh and down across the rolling grasslands that fronted the city of Damascus to the west.

There was no haste in them. Samarkand lay half a world away. They let their horses drink in the cold, flowing waters of the Litany, and here also they washed hands and faces, and lay in the river grasses chewing on a roasted wild hog that had fallen to John of Lincoln's long sword as it came grunting out of the reeds.

Their second night was much like the first, but now Shirzade sat with her arm touching his, and the perfume of her thick black hair was close and intoxicating. The Crusader found that his heart hammered whenever she shifted her weight so that her soft hip bulged warm against him.

She sang to him softly in strange words, the *mu'allaqa* of the poet Imru'l-Qais, and the Sirat 'Antar. As she sang these rich poems, she translated them into the lingua franca.

The night was cold and dark, but its air was filled with fragrance, and the fire was a warm, living thing before them. For the first time in his life the Crusader was being offered something other than the clang of weapons, the dust of battle against the paynim hordes, and the stern discipline of Templar ranks. A woman had never leaned against him and sang of love to his ears as this one did, with her flesh soft and her perfume all around him. She wove a spell with the words she sang, and with her gentle camaraderie.

When she leaned on his arm to rise to her feet and seek her sheepskins, he rose with her, still in the spell of her words and laughter. Almost unconsciously his arm tightened around her sinuous waist, making her sway toward him. Her dark eyes sought his, and now the laughter in them was gone, replaced by a glowing challenge that made the Crusader tremble.

"You have not yet caught me after the feasting, *bagatur!*" she whispered. It was not until long weeks later that he was to learn the meaning of her words. She released herself gently.

An hour after dawn they were splashing across a narrow ford of the river Litany, up onto a gravelly bank, to clatter beyond a sloping ridge that was dotted with ilex.

The gradual ascent to the mountain pass of the Jebel Keniseh rose steeply, traversing a twisting path between sheer shoulders of bald-faced rock. Toward noon they came out onto the wider courier road from the little goat path they had been following. A thousand feet ahead of them, like a slice wedged from the mountainside, was the pass.

They were halfway through the gorge, galloping with a jangle of bridle bits and with saddle leather creaking under them, when they heard a horn braying.

John of Lincoln had heard those musical notes before. He reined in and his hand fell to the worn handle of his spiked ball.

"A paynim oliphant. The war horn of Imadeddin Zengi!"

Chapter Seven

THE YOUNG SELJUK CAPTAIN rode with anger in his heart. Behind him, a file of mounted swordsmen and archers spurred at the gallop to keep pace with his roan gelding, for Nasran ibn-Afdal ran with the careless fury of those in whom emotion had replaced reason. Behind him he left a young wife newly wedded in the great mosque of Aleppo, for when the Atabeg of Mosul beckoned, young captains did not dally. And so Nasran ibn-Afdal rode with the wind on his cheeks and red rage under his chain mail.

It was that fury that made him order the oliphant sounded when a distant scout signaled back that his keen eyes had sighted their prey.

Nasran ibn-Afdal allowed himself the luxury of a small smile. By the beard of the Prophet, it would be sooner ended than he'd dared hope! His separation from the modishly plump Zobeibe would not be long endured. The little absence might even add flavor to their next meeting. And so Nasran ibn-Afdal lifted his right hand high and swung it forward, and himself led the upward run of his mailed cohorts toward the mountain pass of the Jebel Keniseh.

Far ahead of them the Moslem riders could see the four fugitives bent forward in their saddles, their mounts lifting tiny puffs of dry dust with their pounding hoofs. The wind of their passage between the high screes and tumbled clumps of talus rippled the long gray abas streaming out behind them.

Two of the fugitives were turning and standing on their stirrups, bringing their short bows upward from the bow cases at their left hips. Now they were fitting black arrow shafts to the strings, drawing and releasing them.

A shaft whirled overhead, missing the young emir, but he could hear the gurgled scream of a man who had caught that Mongol arrowhead deep in his windpipe. A second man slid from his saddle and bounced twice when he hit the ground.

"*Wallahi!*" grunted the Emir. "Are those little men jinn that their every shaft finds a target?"

Two more men fell from the ranks of the oncoming

riders. With a lump in his throat that was the pride he was swallowing, Nasran ibn-Afdal waved a mailed arm.

"Fan out! Fan out and split apart. Up shields! Catch those arrows as they come down."

It was easy advice, but it was midmorning and those shafts came down out of the sun, and no man had an eye so swift that he could gauge their flight. It was all a man could do to crouch behind his shield and ride blindly, hoping that Allah in His mercy would veil his flesh from those all-seeing points.

The arrows delayed the Moslem riders, but not for long.

Nasran ibn-Afdal would not let his men turn aside. He stood in his iron stirrups and his loud sneer carried downwind to every ear. "O True Believers! Am I to return to our little father, the great Atabeg, and tell him two half-grown men with bows in their fists defeated us?"

His men roared in their shame, and in that instant of their anger he sent them forward, scimitars out and flashing, in a line of hurtling horseflesh that drove the dust upward in a great yellow cloud.

The delay had given the two little men, and the tall Crusader and the veiled woman who rode with them, an opportunity to move out of the pass and gallop downslope toward a beetling knoll of chalky limestone.

Here the big Crusader came to his feet and, lifting the woman down, helped her to the flat top of the mound. Then he swung a great round ball that was set with spikes about his head, so that Nasran ibn-Afdal could hear it whistling even above the thunder of hoofs on the limestone floor.

On either side of him the two Mongol archers stood, loosing their arrows. Man after man tumbled from the leather saddles as those shafts found mail chinks, or drove with stunning force through iron mesh and leather jacket.

They swarmed around the knoll, but it was higher than a tall man, and the Seljuk swordsmen of Mosul had to go up it on foot. Nasran ibn-Afdal hurled a hundred scimitars forward and sat back with both hands resting on his ivory pommel, smiling and thinking of the plump Zobeibe.

He did not sit there long.

A great spiked ball hurtled like the fist of some mighty jinn, and where it went, men crumpled before its sweep.

It danced above the rim of the little hill, and when it came down, men died silently, or fell screaming with faces punctured by those scraping spikes. Beside the Crusader fought a woman in sheepskin trousers and a brocade jacket, her cloak discarded to free an arm for the swing of her curving blade.

On the other side of the knoll the Mongols fought, dark little men with their eyes alight with battle lust. They were agile as monkeys, running here, then there, to cover their half of the little tableland.

Steel scraped on steel. Booted feet stamped thick dust over tumbling stones and gravel. Men panted in the cool mountain air, and sweat ran down into their eyes.

A score of his swordsmen lay inert at the foot of the knoll before Nasran ibn-Afdal became aware of the stand these four were making. He jerked erect against the cantle of his saddle, eyes widening.

"Hai," he muttered in admiration. "The infidels fight as if they were children of the Prophet!"

Almost reluctantly he waved the mounted archers forward.

Turkish bows swung free, great bent weapons formed of sinew and wood and horn in layers that could drive an arrow more than eight hundred yards. Arrows came out of wooden bow cases and were notched to gut strings. The bows bent back, then spanged forward.

A hail of feather shafts swept the knoll. Three of them drove into the body of the Mongol Sofodai, so that he fell face down over the edge of the knoll, dead before he hit the ground. The other Mongol clawed helplessly at a transfixed throat, knees bending, crumpling where he stood.

Two shafts bounded off the armor of John of Lincoln.

Shirzade screamed once, but it was a scream of horror at sight of her falling Mongols, rather than a scream of pain. Under threat of death by dismemberment, the Moslem archers had been ordered not to hit her.

John of Lincoln picked up his great shield and strapped it to his arm. There were no more arrows, but now the paynim swordsmen were swarming up over the rim of the knoll and heading for him.

He looked into the wide, frightened eyes of the Persian woman. "It will be a fight they will speak of to their grandchildren," he promised her, and went to meet them.

His great spiked mace leaped and twirled. It went out to the length of its chain and it screamed as it came down in a bloody arc against the Seljuks. His shield caught thrusting scimitars, turning them. The horn handle of his weapon jumped and throbbed in his big mailed hand as he sent the mace swirling and darting out before him.

Shirzade watched a moment, then lifted the scimitar that had been forged in the armory fires at Damascus and brought by caravan to Samarkand. With it straight before her, she went running into the men who sought to take the Crusader at his back.

These men had been warned by the young emir. This woman was inviolate, holy. They fell away, letting her put her back to the shoulders of John of Lincoln.

"We die together, man of the red cross!" she panted, eyes glinting hard at the dismayed Seljuks.

But John of Lincoln needed room in which to swing that mace and chain. The woman at his back was a hindrance. As if realizing this, she moved forward a few steps, scimitar uplifted.

As they paused there, a horn sounded from the slopes below.

Nasran ibn-Afdal reined his roan gelding around. In the sunlight flooding the eastern face of the Jebel Keniseh he saw a great host of soldiers spurring hard.

They bore small round shields and yard-long straight swords. They rode with the wind whipping their mail kepis back from gleaming spiked helmets. Three silken banners, ornate with the religious symbols of Mohammed, floated high on tall poles.

Nasran ibn-Afdal knew those banners. Serving under Imadeddin Zengi, he had met them in battle at the siege of Damascus less than a year before.

"Unur's men!" he told the air around him.

The old Mameluke had sent more than three times his own force on this foray. Already his archers were putting shafts in the air, and men were dying under them. For a moment Nasran ibn-Afdal hesitated, remembering the anger of his atabeg. He could hurl his men against the Damascenes, but they would be swallowed up and destroyed. Better to retreat now, to fight another time.

The war horns sounded the recall, and in another moment the Crusader and Shirzade stood alone.

Though Nasran ibn-Afdal was content to run before

the host of Unur, the young emir Ramid ibn-Ghazi was not so disposed to let him go. He hurled his warriors after the fleeing Seljuks.

They met in a clang of steel and harsh cries at the mouth of the narrow mountain pass. Dust swirled up like a saffron veil to hide the play of scimitar and sword, the clangor of blades meeting ·shield bosses, the moans of dying men. The noises hung there in the dust for a little while, and then the wind stirred through the pass and blew the dust away, and the pass was empty of all but dead men lying on the stones. The sound of battle came back only faintly from the deeper recesses of the mountain pathway.

Shirzade wept a little over her dead Mongols, with the big Crusader standing grim and bloody in his battered chain mail above her. When he had let her cry softly for a little while, he put a hand to her shoulder.

"They'll be coming back. Those who rescued us were Musselmen, just as were Zengi's men. They won't be our friends."

"They were the soldiers of Damascus," said the Persian: "I've seen those banners hanging on the palace walls."

She let him bring her down from the knoll and to her palfrey. He held the iron stirrup as she slid the dusty toe of her red leather boot into it and rose to the saddle.

They put spurs to their mounts, clattering down the stony hillside, galloping over the shoulder of a rocky ridge, moving between great limestone boulders and clumps of shattered marl.

It seemed for a moment, as they drove past a thin tongue of rock that lifted like a brown finger into the air, that they would get away. But a voice hallooed, and as John of Lincoln turned, he saw a score of riders blocking them.

As they reined in, the emir Ramid ibn-Ghazi let his eyes assess the woman in the dusty brocade jacket. He saw how lean was her waist, and the thrusting prominence of her *salta* bodice. The legs below the hem of the *salta* were as shapely as those of a houri. Ramid ibn-Ghazi smiled to himself.

He made an obeisance to the woman, his gaze finding her sloe eyes. He said mockingly, "I saw that you were anxious to get away, but I came to bid you wait. I can offer you the escort of a thousand Damascus swordsmen. You'll be safe with them."

As he stared into the mocking eyes of this dark-skinned emir, John of Lincoln felt fury flaring in him. The impulse to smash his big fist into that smiling face was something he had to fight to overcome. And so, to give his muscles play, he kneed Thane forward, so that the big Templar horse could shoulder the smaller Arab stallion away from the bay mount that Shirzade straddled.

That Ramid ibn-Ghazi felt the challenge of the Frank was evidenced by the hiss of breath through his thin lips. Anger grew in his dark eyes, and he sat straighter in the ivory saddle. Frank and emir locked eyes, and in that instant each knew the other for an enemy that only death could reconcile.

Ramid ibn-Ghazi regarded the Crusader curiously. Tales had come to the walls of the mosques concerning this yellow-haired Frank giant who fought with a metal ball fitted with spikes. His eyes touched those spikes now, and mentally hefted the big ball and chain. The man must be a veritable Jamshid to wield such a weapon!

"There'll be safe conduct for your infidel paladin, too," he taunted, "if he fights as well as the dead Seljuks below the knoll seem to attest. Unur can use such a one."

John of Lincoln growled, "We need no escort! We ride to the caravanserai of Damascus, to take the camel train to Baghdad. From Baghdad we go on to Samarkand."

The young emir bowed his head slightly. Let the infidel fool believe what he would. He would not waste the breath of a True Believer in argument with him.

He waved a hand and the riders fell in behind him.

"I myself will escort you to the tents."

The Crusader looked at Shirzade. His hand was wrapped around the horn handle of his mace-and-chain. He was willing to fight again, one against twenty. Only her eyes must speak and give him the word.

The Persian woman shook her head so that her veil rippled.

"Let us ride with our new friend, Yukhannan. With him we will be safe from Imadeddin Zengi and his Seljuks."

They cantered down the hills of the Jebel Keniseh, Ramid ibn-Ghazi and John of Lincoln flanking Shirzade on either side, with hatred building between them.

As they passed a clump of limestone that bordered the ridge they rode, the mountain fell away before their eyes. Their eyes took in the tents set up in the valley below. They were the coned, silken tents of the Damascenes, their poletops fitted with metal crescents winking in the sun, their silken sides red and green and yellow. Spread in a circle across one corner of the valley, they gave the impression of strange and alien blossoms lushly sprawling.

Before he dismounted at the scarlet flaps of his commander's baldachin, Ramid ibn-Ghazi said to the Persian woman, "I will have your tent prepared, *yah sitt*. There will be slave women to attend your needs, and silks and velvets from Marv and Shushtar in which to wrap yourself."

His eyes glowed as if at a mental picture of that dressing. John of Lincoln growled at him, for he himself was bothered by that same imagery, and it angered him that this paynim emir should visualize what he could see so clearly.

Then a slave was at the stirrup of the Crusader, and when he was dismounted the slave led him between the rows of silken canopies to a small tent. There were rugs on the bare dirt floor, and vessels of copper and enamelwork, ewers containing water and flagons of date wine. A little fire glowed in a black iron brazier.

The servant—a slave from the Circassus—bowed him through the open flaps. "The emir Ramid commands me to your wish, master," he said softly. "Shall I bring warmed water and a tub?"

John of Lincoln began to unstrap his armor, nodding at the servant.

"Warm water," he said, sighing, "and a big tub."

"It shall be done, *yah khwaja*."

Soon he was naked in the tent, moving a soft cloth thick with suds over his ribs and belly, and down the long legs that were hard with muscles. The grime and the dirt fell from him, leaving his skin whitely pink, except for the dark sun brown that coated his neck and face and his big hands.

He took the soft towels that the Circassan gave him, and when he had dried himself he donned loose black trousers and a *djebba* of white wool. With a cloth-of-gold sash, he selected knee-high boots of the yellow leather of Aleppo. When the Circassan brought him a polished

steel mirror in which to study himself, he discovered that
he looked almost as much the Moslem noble as did
Ramid ibn-Ghazi, except for his poll of yellow hair.

Ramid ibn-Ghazi reclined on the cushions of his great
tent and watched the scented blue smoke of the Tibetan
incense that burned in the silver *tuyère* on the small table before him. His slitted eyes followed the drifting
cloud, seeing in its swirling mist the ivory body of the
Persian princess from the Khorosan steppes. His ruddy
lips curled in a dreaming smile.

Outside the tent, the normal sounds of a Moslem camp
came to his ears. A horse trumpeted angrily. A sledge
beat rhythmically against the blade of a scimitar over an
anvil. The clang and thud of marching men were faint
with distance. Somewhere men laughed in their excitement as they followed the play of carved wooden chess
figures on a checkered board.

The young emir was warm with food and with the
headiness of Yazd wine. His cheeks were warm, almost
hot. The Princess Shirzade had been enchantingly distant over the hot kebab and Syrian figs at the evening
meal. Her eyes had gone again and again to the Crusader,
uncomfortable and ill at ease in his unfamiliar *djebba*
and loose woolen trousers.

"She loves him," Ramid ibn-Ghazi told the incense.
"*Mashallah!* What a waste of woman flesh!" The young
emir conceived himself a very *kadi* where it came to
women.

He lay back, toying with the idea of summoning the
coppery slave girl Ilika. But he had spent the last five
nights with the Danishmend girl, and she was beginning
to pall. It was more fun to lie here and think about the
woman of the far steppes.

The incense was cloying. It made him drowsy. For a
little while he dozed, there in his sumptuous baldachin,
and his snores blew out and away, past the motionless
guards at the closed flaps.

The moon was high in the night heavens when Ramid
ibn-Ghazi woke and came to the opening of his tent. He
breathed in the cool wind, smelling the scent of flowering
evergreens it carried from the nearby hills. The young
emir found himself wide awake, refreshed and strong as
a youthful lion after a kill. Vigor made him stretch his

legs and his arms, and as he brought his arms down, his eyes sought the scarlet tent he had assigned to the Persian woman.

Beyond those red silk walls she dreamed in sleep. There would be a thin wrap over her body and her thick black hair would be a carpet across her pillow. Ramid ibn-Ghazi touched his ruddy lips with a thoughtful tongue.

He whispered to the guard, "Follow me!" and then he went striding between the silken tents, his striped *khalat* fluttering behind him.

With a sweep of an arm he lifted the tent flap and stared in at a little bronze lamp, whose palm-oil flame flickered brightly in the rush of outer air. Shirzade lay on her side under a light woolen *shama*.

Ramid ibn-Ghazi caught his breath. His eyes glowed as they ran up and down that sleeping body, from the pale feet to the crown of heavy black hair. He stepped quickly inside the tent, so that the silken flap fell and hid him in its shadow.

On silent feet he went forward to tower above this princess from Samarkand. Ramid ibn-Ghazi knelt and put out a hand to the woman.

Chapter Eight

Shirzade felt a hard palm on her mouth. Torn from the webbing of her dreams, she thought at first it was her Crusader knight who knelt above her. Her sloe eyes widened lazily, and she stirred against the pressure of the hand, turning her head.

When she recognized the Emir and heard the breath that rasped in his swelling throat, she opened her mouth.

Ramid ibn-Ghazi felt her lips widen, felt part of his hand go into her yawning mouth. And then he stiffened in agony, for instead of the soft pressure of her lips, he felt the edges of sharp white teeth.

Shirzade bit down hard on that palm. Against her lips she tasted hot blood, and she laughed low in her throat.

The Emir yanked his hand back, whispering, "By the beard! Have I caught a tigress?"

His hand throbbed where she had set her teeth, but he almost forgot that pain as she twisted away from him so that the white woolen *shama* came down to the middle of her ivory back.

Ramid ibn-Ghazi lunged at her. His hand caught the glossy black hair that hung over her shoulders, jerking her toward him. She turned then, and her long fingernails clawed at his bearded face. They panted harshly, rolling over the carpets strewn across the hard bare ground of the tent floor.

The Emir was a man used to the saddle and the camps of battle. His muscles were like thin steel. Slowly he bent the Khorosan backward, imprisoning her wrists in his hands. A triumphant smile spread across his dark face, revealing his white teeth.

"*Mashallah!*" he swore hotly. "What a little tiger cat! No wonder Unur is so eager to own you!"

The little Danishmend slave girl Ilika could not sleep. She tossed and writhed on her silken cushions, aware that she had wasted time by perfuming her hair and tinting the tips of her fingers with henna. With care she had chosen the silks that she wore on her coppery legs and bosom, in order that she might bring a hungry look to the eyes of her lord, the Emir.

Ilika hit the cushion beside her with a tiny fist.

"Instead of me, he wants the barbarian, that woman from Samarkand!"

She could not sleep. She got to her bare feet and moved to the open flaps of her conical tent. In the shadows outside she saw a big man standing, a man in black trousers and striped woolen *djebba*. The head that was bared to the night winds shone a pale gold in the moonlight.

"The Frangi warrior," she whispered. "He stands there listening to Ramid and that trousered harlot!"

Ilika smiled thinly. This man was bigger than the Emir. He was almost like a giant to the slave girl, who was used to the smaller Moslem men. With his bare hands he would be able to lift the Emir and strangle him.

The scarlet toes of the slave girl kicked dust as she sidled into the moonlight between the tents, to stand beside the big Crusader. With her head tilted to one side, she smiled up at him.

"He is in her tent, Frangi," she whispered. "You could go in there, if someone were to keep the tent guard busy in talk."

John of Lincoln scowled at the slim girl. Her Arabian perfumes were musky in the night. Beneath her plucked brows, her brown eyes were brightly curious. He said, "Do you hate him?"

"Oh, no. I wouldn't want you to hurt him. Not hurt him too much, that is. If he should not be able to talk for a day or two, though—just to teach him not to go into strange girls' tents!—I would not be unhappy."

She giggled, and the big Crusader grinned at her. He whispered, "Talk to the guard, little one. I'll slip under a fold of the tent between the stakes. I won't hurt your man. Not too much, anyhow!"

"Go with Allah, Frangi," said the girl, and padded off into the shadows.

John of Lincoln moved like a bulky black shadow himself, bent forward with his large hands dangling. He lowered himself flat on his belly and wriggled forward under the folds of the silken canopy, strangely eager to have that throat helpless in his long fingers.

In the flickering light of the palm-oil brass lamp he could see the Emir struggling with the Princess Shirzade. His face was dark with fury, and there was blood on the palm of his hand.

As he watched, Shirzade relaxed, her muscles unequal to the task she set them. And as she went back, the Emir lunged forward.

It was then that John of Lincoln moved. He tore his shadow from the darker shadows behind him and his sandaled feet made no sound on the thick Tiberian carpets. His big hands came down on either side of the Emir's neck and his long brown fingers closed down hard.

Those hands were like an iron collar around the throat of Ramid ibn-Ghazi. He stiffened, releasing the woman, clawing at those fingers that went deeper and deeper into his flesh. Sweat came out on his forehead. His eyes began to throb and protrude.

The hands lifted him, held him high.

And then, as he writhed and kicked, sobbing to draw air into his tortured lungs, the hands let him go.

A fist hurtled through the air. It thudded against the Emir, high on his temple. He fell as a poled ox might fall, limp and boneless.

For an instant John of Lincoln stared down at him. The Emir would have difficulty in talking for perhaps three or four days. The little slave girl would have a good time, nursing him back to health.

The Crusader looked at the woman from Samarkand.

In her excitement, Shirzade forgot that all she wore was the fleecy *shama* that lay crumpled now on the cushions. Leaning forward on a slim ivory arm, she had watched with wide eyes as the Frank lifted the Emir high with astonishing ease. The heavy blow he struck had made a dull sound in the tent, causing her to wince.

As her champion turned to stare at her, Shirzade almost squealed. Her slim fingers hunted frantically for the *shama,* lifting it to hide herself. Over its fringed edge she regarded John of Lincoln with wide eyes.

Now for the first time the Crusader saw her face. It was oval and warmly flushed, her ivory cheeks stained a delicate pink. The long-lashed black eyes were steady, and not at all ashamed. Thick black hair flooded down over her smooth shoulders. As he had thought, her red mouth was a wide, soft bow above her dimpled chin.

Shirzade said, "He will kill you for hitting him! As I would have killed myself, if he had—overcome me."

John of Lincoln was aware that his face was red. He said as he turned his back, "Put on your clothes. Your old clothes, the *tschim* and the *salta*. We will ride to Damascus now."

"He will only follow and take us again."

"I promised his slave girl I wouldn't hurt him too much. But still, he'll be in no condition to give orders for a few hours. I think the slave girl will help us get away, if only to be rid of you."

Behind his back, the Khorosan smiled. She dropped the shielding *shama* and caught up her garments. Swiftly she dressed, aware that he stood like a stone boulder, unmoving, though he must see her shadow where the palm-oil lamp threw it against a silken tent wall. His very immobility gave her a sort of strength.

She came quietly to his side, touching his arm.

With the putting on of his striped *djebba* and his loose black trousers, John of Lincoln was discovering that he was discarding the old habits of his life. There was a looseness to these garments that seemed to symbolize a wild freedom. He felt drunk with it as it hummed in his veins, fueled by the soft warmth of this woman.

Almost savagely he thrust his arm around her waist and pulled her to him. In that same movement, his right hand went up to her face veil and tore it from her head-cloth. He bent to kiss her, finding her mouth half open and fragrant, and sweet as a Malban fig. With fierce hunger he fed on her lips, imprisoning her with arms that were like metal bands around her back, until he had to let her go in order to gulp air into his heaving lungs.

She whispered, "You make love the way you fight, *bagatur!*" But she did not seem to be displeased.

They would have sought the strange elixir of that kiss again had not the tent flap lifted to reveal the little slave girl Ilika. Her eyes slid anxiously across the carpeted tent floor to the inert Ramid ibn-Ghazi, and when she heard him groan, she smiled. Even from where she stood, she could see the dark blue bruises on his throat. Ramid ibn-Ghazi would not soon be so eager to test a stranger's virtue!

Ilika whispered, "I have your horses saddled and ready to run. They've been fed and watered and washed and curried. I've tied waterskins to the saddle pommels, with sacks of fruit beside them, and the infidel's big spiked ball."

She took them between dark tents until they were close to the edge of the camp, and when the guards moved forward with light spears held diagonally across their chests, she extended a forefinger on which glinted a gold ring. At sight of that ring, the guards stepped aside, salaaming.

John of Lincoln assisted the Princess into her saddle. Then he put a foot to his stirrup and swung up into his own kak.

"Will he harm you, little one?" asked Shirzade. "You could come with us."

Ilika shrugged a shoulder. "He'll pout and have the vapors for a few days, but I'll soon convince him I did the wise thing in letting you go. Unur wants you, Woman of the Steppes. It was for Unur that Ramid rode with a thousand men. If he had—taken you, Unur would have had him flayed alive for a full week in the great square at Damascus!" The little slave girl laughed angrily. "Old Unur is a goat who's forgotten his age, but he can be handled. Ramid ibn-Ghazi is not so easy to checkrein, because he is younger and not so impatient of time. Go you with Allah."

John of Lincoln asked no further blessing. As he brought his palm flat across the rump of the bay horse, he toed the black stallion forward. Side by side he and the Princess Shirzade galloped across grasses that were purple under the glittering stars toward the towered city of Damascus.

As he toed his little mule through the narrow gorge that was the courier road from Beirut to Damascus, Ahmed the Assassin saw the buzzards. He watched them curiously, wondering at their food, until he whipped the mule out onto the slopes of the Jebel Keniseh and saw the Seljuks dead in their armor by the little knoll.

He sat his saddle a moment, staring down at the two fallen Mongol archers. Then he gathered his black wool caftan with the red stripes about him, to dismount and go from dead man to dead man, driving off the feeding buzzards. Carefully he examined every face, every body, noting the size of the boot marks in the brown dust.

A wry smile twisted Ahmed's wide mouth as he stood erect and looked from the knoll down across the valley at the coned tents of the Mamelukes from Damascus. A stray breeze plucked at the hairs of his pointed brown beard.

"Allah is good to His humble servant," he whispered. "The Frangi is not among the slain. He must be yonder, in those tents."

The Assassin climbed up onto his mule and toed it forward.

Chapter Nine

HAJJI THE *mukowam*, the camel master, lowered the wet mouth of the waterskin from his mouth and sighed gustily. With the dark brown woolen sleeve of his *kasabia* he wiped the red wine of Shiraz from his lips. He stood near the latticed stone grille of the caravanserai in Damascus. For twenty years Hajji had guided caravans from this tiled and gilded khan eastward to Baghdad across the vast wastes of the *badiyah*. He knew the heat of the red desert sands by day, and their cold at night. Some men said he could even talk to the dust devils that killed men by filling their lungs so they could not breathe.

Hajji thought about the desert, and made a wry face. He shook the goatskin bladder. A faint gurgle answered his move. "*Y'Allah*," he said to the sagging *kirba*, "it will be a long, hot journey! A man must fortify himself against all that heat and sand!"

And so Hajji lifted the goatskin once more to his mouth.

He paused with the waterskin held like that, his eyes opening wide. "By Ansur's curse," he whispered, "never before has the wine of Shiraz done this to my wits. I see a houri. A houri from paradise!"

She was no dead houri, this woman who reined in her bay horse in the shadows of the tiled caravanserai. A veil fluttered down over the bridge of her nose as if to hurried breathing and the dark eyes above the yashmak were bright with life, veiled with long lashes. Her *salta* clung to her slim middle and generous breasts. The thighs with which she gripped the red leather saddle of her bay horse were shapely beneath her *tschim*.

A big man rode a black stallion beside the woman. From what Hajji could see of his bronzed face under the hood of his barracan, he seemed a surly devil. But with red wine in his belly, Hajji was no questioning *kadi*. He bowed low to the woman, and gestured at the row of kneeling camels that stretched under the low arches of the khan as far as the open courtyard beyond the stone staircase leading to the upper stories.

"May I serve you as the Prophet served Allah, O Delight to the Eyes." Hajji belched, attempting a bow.

"You are the caravan leader? The *bashi?*"

"*Bashi* and *mukowam,*" grumbled Hajji, "and anything else that concerns the caravan. But we do not travel swiftly. If it's haste you want, the courier road by the wells of Melossa to Kubaisa would better suit your purpose. I guide a slow *kafila* to Rutba, and on to Ramadi."

"You talk with a tongue well oiled by the juice of grapes, Father of Windbags," said the woman, tossing a plump leather purse through the air. "Give us our position, that we may rest until the dawn departure."

Hajji bobbed his gray head until his turban tassels swung wildly. "You shall be given a good post, *yah sitt.* In the middle of the *kafila,* between the spice camels of Mahmoud ben-Rahman and the slave girls of Yazid ibn-Hayyan, the Armenian."

The old caravan leader watched the man and woman walk their horses past the piled bales of silks and brocades. Their footfalls echoed in the high groined ceiling with its arched columns and spacious balconies. The tinkle of the great fountain came to old Hajji then, and made his lips twitch. He swung the mouthpiece of his wineskin to his mouth and threw his head far back.

John of Lincoln chuckled, turning his head to watch him. "He's almost as round as that wineskin when it's full. If he can guide a caravan to Baghdad as well as he guides that bladder mouthpiece to his lips, we're as good as in Samarkand already."

Her little hand was warm as her fingers tightened on his arm. "No talk of Samarkand, Yukhannan! Remember what I told you. You are my chief eunuch, bringing me back to my husband after a pilgrimage to Mecca."

"Chief eunuch!" he snorted, eying her as she swung from the bay horse to unwrap her sleeping woolens and spread them under a window latticework.

Shirzade giggled. "Bestir yourself, Yukhannan. We don't have many hours of sleep left to us. Dawn comes early to the khan."

She was stretching out on the thick gray wool of her barracan as she spoke, turning to draw its fleecy folds around her shoulders. For a moment John of Lincoln stared, then swung down and lifted off both saddles and bridles. He fed and watered the horses at the great fountain near the trading blocks, and tied them to iron wall rings with rope hackamores.

Then he stretched out on his own barracan, close to Shirzade. Faintly, as the gathering dusk grew to darkness, he could hear the soft blowings of the tethered camels, the snores of their drivers, the voices of the sellers of wares and foodstuffs in the distant *sûks*. They made a rhythmic drone that lulled the Crusader to sleep. His last thought as he closed his eyes was that he would hear many new and strange sounds before he sighted the high walls of Samarkand.

Caravans have crossed the great desert of Syria since man first tied a pannier to the back of a camel. For centuries those shaggy beasts have laid the marks of their pads from Aleppo to Basra, from Palmyra south to Mecca. As others had done before him, Hajji moved his camels out at dawn, with the wind whipping up the cobblestoned streets of the ancient city to stir the fringes of the *mohaffas* and ruffle the camels' dangling red cheek tassels. Like some great brown serpent the caravan filed past the long canals and wound in and around the Street of the Great Mosque.

Moving out the Caravan Gate, they swung southeastward, crawling steadily across the shale ground of the *kafila* road to Dumier. In the distance the Jebel Rawak lifted its brown bulk upward from the level plain. With the sun red in their eyes at first, then growing into a mighty golden ball flooding the brassy sky with radiance, they crawled onward. Tinkling camel bells made weird music as the huge palanquins, swathed in muslin and shaped like cones of sherbet around the tall pannier poles, bobbed and dipped to every stride.

John of Lincoln rode stirrup to stirrup with the veiled Shirzade as they walked their horses between the baggage camels of Mahmoud ben-Rahman, who was carrying spices and essences from Cairo to Mosul, and the gilded *mohaffas* of the Armenian Yazid ibn-Hayyan, whose women were destined for the slave marts of Basra.

Less than five days ago the big Crusader would have known horror at the thought that he rode with a woman away from the Holy Land toward the steppes of central Asia. Now, he reflected as he clattered Thane over a river bridge, he was discovering something wild and untamed in him that made him grin at the thought. He supposed it had something to do with the loose *djebba* and black wool trousers he wore, and the hooded gray

barracan over his head. Looking like a paynim, he felt
himself infected with their philosophies.

All that first morning the caravan walked through a
cloud of drifting dust, with the camel drivers chanting
the *huda* and the copper bells eternally sounding in the
dun mists. As it slithered deeper onto the vast stony plateau that stretched to the Euphrates, the *kafila* left the
familiar world behind and gathered around itself the
sounds of camels blowing, the cries of their drivers, the
faint babble of voices muted by the wind. The sky lowered to press its heat down on them as the horizons widened on every side.

Past midday they halted at a mud-brick khan to water
the animals and give cramped muscles a chance to stretch.
Shirzade drew John of Lincoln with her to a little space
where she knelt to draw a map on the hard-packed
ground with her slim dagger.

"We ride south of the usual caravan routes, Yukhannan. We travel by way of the wells of Rutba, rather than
by the faster courier route to Bir Melossa and Kubaisa.
If Unur or Imadeddin Zengi send men after us, they
will never suspect we have come this far off the usual
desert roads. They will look for us around Bir Melossa.
or possibly Palmyra to the north."

John of Lincoln listened to a camel bray softly as he
lifted his chest to drink in the dry desert air. "By the
time they have searched every caravan between Damascus and Ramadi, we'll be riding through Baghdad!"

It was in that spirit of renewed hope that they mounted
and fell into line behind the baggage camels of Mahmoud
ben-Rahman and the *mohaffas* of the Armenian Yazid
ibn-Hayyan. From this watering stop to Rutba wells lay
more than two hundred miles of shale and sand. The sky
was a blue haze overhead, and as the hot desert wind
whipped across their faces it seemed that this new world
through which they rode was blowing them a welcome.

"A new world that will adopt us," the Crusader told
Shirzade, putting a palm on her thigh. "A world we'll
make our own."

He felt her thigh muscles tighten under his hand, and
saw the manner in which her gaze sought his face. John
of Lincoln grinned to himself and let his thoughts dwell
on the coming night serai, and of how her mouth might
taste in the shadow of a desert khan's mud-brick wall.

The little slave girl Ilika sat back on her heels and frowned behind the back of Ramid ibn-Ghazi. All this morning he had been a wildman, asking Allah to put the yellow-haired Crusader in his hands, promising gifts of silver statues and salvers of gold from the *sûk* of the artisans for the mosques at Mecca.

"Just once to lay my steel on his white skin!" he fumed, striding from the tent pole to the *diwan*, past the rack that held his weapons. "I'll heat a dagger and burn my name in his belly! I'll have the skin flayed from his back. Eh, Ibrahim?"

The tall slave who stood in the tent mouth bowed low, touching heart and lips and head in the graceful *temena*. "An Ismailite named Ahmed, Highness. He seeks the white Frangi we rescued yesterday."

Ramid grimaced. He had no love for these Assassins who crept like poisonous snakes from city to city on the trail of some poor devil marked for an early grave. "He seeks the Frangi, does he? Show him in!" He whirled on the Danishmend girl and growled, "You saw them ride off, Ilika?"

"Yes, *yah khwaja!* They rode to Damascus."

Ramid ibn-Ghazi smiled agreeably, showing small teeth above his curled and scented beard. "Ah, yes. Damascus!"

Ahmed the Assassin salaamed low before the Emir, apologizing for disturbing the serenity of this highborn noble with his unworthy presence. He pleaded for his help to track down an infidel who had lived too long and merited death so that his feet could no longer pollute the sacred sands of the lands of Mohammed. Ramid ibn-Ghazi listened with a smile twitching his full mouth.

The Emir broke in with a wave of an impatient hand. "Yes, yes! I understand you are on a mission. The man you seek rode north, toward Homs."

Ahmed started and eyed the Emir with suspicious eyes. But he could think of no reason why this nobleman should lie to him. He pondered, "North? To Homs? It seems strange."

Ramid shrugged listless shoulders, reaching a hand out for the goblet of rose sherbet the slave girl was handing him. Sipping slowly, he said, "Not so strange, if you consider his reasons. We might expect him to hit for Damascus. But who does he know in the Gateway to the Desert? Is he a True Believer with relatives in the Street of Falling Petals? Or with high connections in the palace? He rides to Homs, to swing east to Palmyra."

"Palmyra," muttered the Assassin. "Christian caravans meet there, traveling south to Basra or north to Aleppo." He broke off, eyes gleaming, smiling faintly. "A thousand blessings on your head, Master of Wisdom," Ahmed murmured, backing out of the tent. "I shall follow him north at the gallop. If I miss him south of Homs, I'll go on to Palmyra. I have—brethren in Palmyra."

Ilika stood up as the tent flap fell behind the Ismailite. She said to the Emir, "You spoke to him with the forked tongue of an infidel, Ramid."

Ramid laughed softly. "Do I want him killing the Crusader before I get my hands on him? Ah, no, little one. When Ramid hates a man, Ramid is jealous of anyone who threatens him. His fate belongs to me."

He put a hand on the soft tresses of the girl where they formed a dark shawl on her shoulders. He went on, "They rode to Damascus, you say. Not having friends there, they will take the first caravan out of the khan. Which way would you travel if you were fleeing Ramid, O Softest of Pillows?"

"If I fled from your anger, yah khwaja," she whispered, "I would flee fast. I would take the courier route to Bir Melossa."

"That is what the Khorosan witch would like me to think," he murmured. "But she'll be clever as a bitch protecting its young. The only other road that any sane person would travel is the route that swings north to Palmyra."

Ilika felt his mouth caressing her neck. She whispered into his ear, "But the Samarkand woman is not sane?"

"She's a devil for sanity. She'll go by the road to the wells of Rutba, by the old Iraki fort. And that is where I'll catch her!"

For a day and a night Ahmed fled like a frightened ghil northward through the schist country of the Jebel Rawak. The hard shale of the old Roman highway would cover the tracks of any horses that had lately galloped here, and so the Ismailite rode without suspicion in him when he found none.

On the morning of the second day, as he rounded a bend in the trail, five helmeted Seljuks waved him to a halt. They brought him to Imadeddin Zengi where he sat an ivory saddle before a detail of his Seljuk swordsmen.

The Seljuk war lord wore a grim frown as he turned from a man who rode beside him, his arm held in a linen sling. His dark brows asked a question of the Ismailite.

"Highness, I seek a Frank warrior."

"So did My Lord Nasran ibn-Afdal! Instead he took a wound from a Mameluke sword!"

The Assassin smiled. "With my own lips I spoke with an emir of Damascus who assured me that the *dair azazil* had ridden north to Homs."

Imadeddin Zengi hit his saddle pommel with a hard palm. "That emir will be the one who raised the swords of his Damascenes against my Seljuks! Nasran ibn-Afdal," and the Seljuk war lord gestured at the flushed face of the man whose arm rested in a sling, "can attest to that! Twice he has failed me!"

The young Seljuk captain growled, "A thousand Mamelukes against two hundred Seljuks, Highness! I brought back half of them!"

Imadeddin Zengi grinned mirthlessly. "Had you brought back the woman, as I ordered, and left the hundred behind, it would have been a price worth paying. Instead, my army is poorer by the hundred you lost."

The Ismailite shifted position. He wanted no part of these Seljuk quarrels. He said softly, "Then Your Worship assures me that the *dair azazil* did not ride north from Damascus?"

Imadeddin Zengi brought his gaze around to rest on the Assassin. "They came not north. My guards have been patrolling the mountain passes for the past two days. The man you hunt probably rode into Damascus, to seek the shelter of a desert caravan."

"Then by your permission, O Giver of Blessings," murmured Ahmed, "I will remove my insignificant self from your illustrious presence. I will—"

The Seljuk war lord halted the Assassin with a wave of the hand. "You'll remain here, close to my warriors. I set out myself with an army to find him and the one who travels with him. When we find the one I seek, you can have the Frangi."

Ahmed might have argued, but there was a hardness to the face of the Seljuk war lord that told him his argument could prove his own death warrant. And so Ahmed, who could bend with a wind where it suited his purpose, only bowed the lower. He whispered, "I am not worthy of the shelter of your grace, Master of Fighting Men. That you should deem me your guest, will comfort me in my aging years."

Imadeddin Zengi snorted, and with the echo of that snort sounding in his ears, Ahmed the Assassin bowed out of his presence. He told himself that he would fare better to ride with this Seljuk escort than alone on his patient mule. He would dine well and drink good wines, and sooner or later they would find the Crusader.

Chapter Ten

THE CARAVAN came down on the little village of dried
mud brick, with its high wall and blooming cactus hedge,
in the cool dusk of early evening. This was their first
encampment since leaving Damascus, and men cried out
harshly to the camels while a fever of impatience ran the
length of the caravan.

Shirzade said, "There will be a rush to find sleeping
space. We would do well to ride ahead, for the ground
around a *kasr* is no respecter of hips and shoulders." She
made a wry face behind her black yashmak. "I've no
desire to test the hardness of the desert stones tonight."

They reined their horses out of line and went galloping past the baggage camels of Mahmoud ben-Rahman.

A dark woman big with child stood close to the wooden
gate of the *kasr*, watching them approach with wide eyes.
As they reined in, horses dancing, John of Lincoln tossed
a silver dinar through the air. The woman seemed not to
move, but her small brown hand flashed out from the
cover of her plain woolen *yelek* to snatch it from a shaft
of dying sunlight.

"Water, woman! Cool water."

The woman looked from the coin to the man and
woman, smiling slightly. "I have fruit juices put away
against the desert heat. Or some *leben,* which is milk
soured and good to the dry throat."

"The fruit juices," decided Shirzade, walking her horse
into the wide court of the caravanserai.

They drank the juices slowly, watching the camels bend
awkwardly as their drivers shouted hoarse commands.
Yazid ibn-Hayyan moved past, with several of his slave
women clad loosely and revealingly in silken transparen-
cies.

Shirzade said softly, as she caught the direction of the
Crusader's gaze, "She is an Arab who will delight the eyes
of some emir in Basra, Yukhannan."

John of Lincoln grinned, and continued to eye the
swinging hips of the lithe Arab whose blued eyes challenged him. He was discovering that his native Lincolnshire had been a cold and harsh country compared to
this hot, dry world. Here the women dared the men,

rather than fleeing from them. For a moment he remembered the Lady Hodierna, and wondered where she was at this instant. From the corner of his eye he caught the movement of Shirzade's shoulder as she shrugged jealously.

He laughed softly and whispered into the ear that lay half hidden beneath her spill of glossy black hair, "You spoke of a sleeping place where the stones would not bruise your flesh, Shirzade. We should go together to find it, as befits a noblewoman and her—eunuch!"

He spilled laughter into her ear, and felt her move against him. She echoed his laughter in her voice as she said, "You're no eunuch, Yukhannan—thank Arsu, god of caravans!"

A handful of silver coins dropped into the calloused palm of the *kasr* woman bought them a spot of ground in the little garden behind the mud-brick house. Here the woman spread a carpet and brought them *sikbaj* stew in round wooden bowls and cold *leben* and cool date wine served in clay goblets.

From somewhere in her house the woman found a *mizafah* and handed it to Shirzade with a curious smile. The Khorosan princess cried out at sight of it, and let her fingertips brush across its strings. Then, with her back propped against the bole of a stunted tamarisk tree, she sang to John of Lincoln of the *khamriyats* of abu-Nuwas, those poetic rhapsodies in which the naughty poet bespoke his love of wine and the pleasures it can induce in a man properly seasoned to its flavors.

As the sky darkened above them and the moon became a great round yellow lantern lifting its rays above the dried mud wall, Shirzade sang more softly. Now she chose the love sonnets of this same abu-Nuwas, the *ghazal,* masterpieces of the erotic and the licentious.

Shadows grew across the garden. Only the silver moonlight was here with them to dapple the ground with faery lacings of silver and black. The caravan sounds were faint, echoes of the day fading away in the darkness of the night.

John of Lincoln lay with his head in her lap, staring upward past the mounds of her bosom at her veil. Almost dreamily he put up a hand and tugged at the black silk. He pulled it free, and as it lay inert across her shoulder he searched the ivory of her face, studying the slim nostrils and the mouth that was full with life and as red as the heart of a blood ruby.

Her mouth opened to her quickened breathing. She felt him stir and sit up with his legs crossed. Then he was reaching for her, drawing her to him, his right arm cradling her weight.

She whispered, "In my country, when a man wants a woman he goes to her family for the wedding feast. When the woman flees, he goes after her. If he catches her, she belongs to him."

He said, "We have feasted on stew and figs. Now I want a richer feast."

His kiss discovered her red mouth to be moist and alive, and as hungry as his own. For a little while they drifted dreamily in fevered caresses, with the wind sighing in the tamarisk branches and the moon a pale weight in the dark desert sky. And then Shirzade drew him closer still and murmured, "This night we need not worry whether there are stones on the ground. We will not feel them."

From the desert *kasr* the caravan crawled eastward into the rising sun. Now the drivers sang the *huda,* the camel song, and the nose fans of the dromedaries bobbed and dipped in tune with the cadenced words. Copper bells and heavy red cheek tassels sang and danced to each swaying stride, and the panniers and *mohaffas* creaked and groaned as the sun grew hotter in the brassy sky.

At midday the caravan crossed the ancient stone road that Roman hands had built from Jauf to Palmyra. The sands sifted across the stone blocks, almost burying them. To either side the brown plains stretched like a dead land whose great sand ridges lay like sere brown bones under the sun. These *dahana* were broken at intervals by chains of jagged rocks from which the branches of thorn scrub and cactus protruded like the withered fingers of buried giants.

Their horses suffered most from the desert crossing, for this was no land for saddle mounts. John of Lincoln and Shirzade dismounted and walked with them at times, going thirsty themselves in order that the black and the bay might gulp at palmsful of water from their leather *kirbas.*

They were deep in the *badiyah* here. The sun on the

barren rocks and shale was a blinding, maddening thing, parching throats and baking men and women slowly. They came to a mineral spring at dusk, and Hajji moved down the line, advising the travelers to fill their emptied waterskins with the bitter waters.

"A few hours' ride will make this water sweet to the tongue. You will think it sugared with the herbs of paradise."

The plump little camelmaster showed no sign of the wines he drank. His nose was bulbous and red above his graying beard, but his eyes were bright and keen. He would pat the wineskins as he rode, estimating out loud just how long they would last him.

"It helps me cross this terrible land," he told John of Lincoln, "as once it helped Omar Khayyam put up with the policies of fools."

From Damascus to the wells of Rutba was a distance of two hundred and fifty miles of loose boulders and sand, silt, and lava. Baggage camels would take ten days for such a trip, barring sandstorm and simoom, Hajji explained. Racing camels could go twice as fast as this, but merchants had no need of dromedaries to transport their spices and silks, slave women and brocades to the *sûks* of Baghdad and Basra.

"Go slow, go sure," Hajji grunted.

The nights grew cold on the desert. In the red fire flame of the camel's-thorn campfires, John of Lincoln found that he was shedding his past with an ease that some months ago would have filled him with unholy horror. He was no longer a Crusader, but a *bagatur*. His body forgot the stifling weight of chain mail and grew accustomed to woolen *djebba* and loose black trousers. And in the nights, with her lap a pillow for his head, he listened to Shirzade recount the endless tales of the Thousand and One Nights. Later, when the caravan was silent around them, he would draw her in against him and feed on her moist red mouth.

The days followed the nights, and now the caravan was less than a day's journey to Rutba wells. The morrow would see the *kafila* split up: part to go east and south, to intersect the great caravan road between Aleppo and Basra, some to move northward and east to Ramadi, and a few others to travel due east to Kerbela, to take the long Darb Zubayda, the pilgrim road to Mecca.

There was to be feasting and dancing on this last night. Bush fires were built in foot-deep holes, and round bread loaves cooked in them.

Mahmoud ben-Rahman brought out three of his slave girls to dance the licentious zarabanda by the red light of the thornbush fires. One of these women was the Arabian whose hips John of Lincoln had admired some nights before. Now, as she danced before the shouting voices of the cameleers and merchants, Shirzade glanced slyly at the big Frank.

"That silk bit she has wrapped around her doesn't hide much," she observed dryly.

His hand sought hers as he murmured, "My eyes have sight only for your beauty, *bayki!*"

To John of Lincoln, here in this little caravanserai half a score of miles from Rutba wells, came the realization that his jesting words were heavy with truth. What had begun as a fascination with the mystery of this veiled woman was now a living hunger for her. He needed no Bishop Gerard or bearded Patriarch of Jerusalem to tell him that all his life he had been seeking her. In cold Norman castles, on the deck of the carrack of the Cinque Ports that had taken him to the Holy Land, in battle after battle with the paynims, a vision of her loveliness had been hidden within him. He had dreamed of her in formless, misty fashion, as some knights had been reputed to glimpse the Grail.

The words would not come with which to tell her of this flaring hunger that possessed him when he looked at her and held her in his arms. He could only draw her tight against him, and breathe in the fragrance of her thick glossy black hair, and know that he needed her.

Womanlike, the Khorosan knew this without being told. Her red mouth curved gently as she leaned her weight to his side and brooded with him at the fire flames and the dancing women. They stood like statues when the roast hare and grouse were passed around on thin sticks, and as the cameleers brought bulging wineskins to gurgle their red contents into little clay drinking cups.

No one noticed when they went, to spread their thick gray barracans beside a flowering acacia. No man heard their whispered voices or saw the lips that kissed hungrily in the stillness of the desert night.

Dawn was tinting the graveled plateau with crimson

flames when John of Lincoln rose to an-elbow, smiling down at the sleeping Shirzade. He bent to kiss her cheek, soft as the petals of a harem rose. Then his gaze lifted to sweep the flat desert.

He saw them then.

A thousand riders strung out behind a man who rode as if a *ghil* howled at his heels. A man in pointed helmet and striped jelab, a man with curled beard and rigid back, whose Damascus blade clanged at every galloping stride of his Arab barb.

Ramid ibn-Ghazi.

Chapter Eleven

Ramid ibn-Ghazi was a baffled man. Under a midday
sun he had gone on foot into the great khan at Damascus, seeking the Crusader knight and the Khorosan princess. From the slave dealers and merchants gathered about
the stalls under the high balconies, he learned that no
such man and woman had been seen.

An opium seller suggested, "They might have sought
caravan space with Hajji, who was bound for Rutba wells
and Ramadi. Perhaps they came at night, so that none
saw their faces, or remembered them."

"It might be as Ali says," added a bearded trader.
"Hajji left at dawn, as any good *bashi* would do. If they
came by darkness and departed in the dawn, who would
see them?"

It was not much, but it would have to do, Ramid realized. He sent Ilika to his marble palace, close to the great
orchards beyond the city, and rode with his thousand
Mamelukes after the caravan of Hajji.

It was a slow process. Horses need care on the desert,
and a thousand horses presented a big problem. Though
the Emir raged, time had to be spent to rest the Arab
mounts and to dig water from ancient wells. And so it
was that not until the tenth morning since leaving Damascus did Ramid ibn-Ghazi sight the resting camels of
Hajji's *kafila*.

He rode directly to the *bashi*, and his voice was sharp
and bitter with the frustration in him as he snapped,
"Eh, *bashi*? Do you have a Christian man and a Khorosan
woman in your party?"

Hajji had drunk well of his wines the night before. His
belly ached with the roast grouse he had consumed, and
he was realizing too late that a man of his advanced years
should not spend so much time with a slave woman, even
such a woman as Yazid ibn-Hayyan had brought by the
hand to him in the light of the dried-dung campfires.

He sighed, remembering the feel of her warm throat
under his palm. He said, "What infidel would ride this
Allah-forsaken wasteland when he has all the Holy Land
to receive his feet?"

"I come for answer, *bashi!* Have you seen them?"

There is no man more exasperating than a caravan leader who chooses to be stupid. Hajji made his shrug a masterpiece of boredom as he said, "Lord, you see the *kafila* before you. Behind you are your Mamelukes. Let them ease their cramping legs by going among my clients. If they find this man and woman, take them. If they do not discover them, let me go on in peace. Already I am late in departing. These delays cost money!"

Ramid ibn-Ghazi eyed the old *bashi* with bright eyes. Nothing would have delighted him more than to bend his scabbard across the fat one's back, but Unur of Damascus would not relish news of such an action. Ramid had done more than enough already to court disfavor with the old Mameluke ruler without risking more.

Ramid stood in his stirrups and waved a score of his riders forward. "Dismount and search the *kafila*," he told them. "A bag of silver dinars to the man who finds the ones I seek."

With grins baring their white teeth, the Mamelukes disappeared among the clustered camels. Cries of outrage and anger rose here and there as rough hands lifted brown woolen hoods to peer intently at dark faces, or tore down face veils to stare at lovely faces.

Yazid ibn-Hayyan defended his slave girls with his armed retainers. Steel clashed and hoarse cries lifted into the growing heat of the desert day. Ramid came spurring up in a cloud of thin dust to drive back his men and demand that he alone view the features of the women bound for the slave marts of Basra.

It was that sudden tumult that gave John of Lincoln the chance he sought. With a hand to restrain the startled Shirzade, he had lain in the shade of the acacia, whispering prayers to the Christus, as the Mamelukes went among the resting camels. Now he rose to his feet and drew the woman with him. On light feet they ran, sheltered by the shaggy brown sides and high palanquins of the baggage camels.

"There is no place to hide," protested the panting Shirzade. "Are you a jinn to make us invisible?"

"Save your breath," the Crusader told her.

They came up on the deserted camels belonging to Hajji in a rush. John of Lincoln found the camel he sought and, lifting the cover of an earthenware wine jug, stooped to peer into the dark interior.

He said, "You've told me tales of your Arabian Nights on the caravanserai stops. I remember a story about forty thieves, and the manner in which they hid in oil jars."

Shirzade gasped and came to stand at his side. "But those jars were empty. These hold the wines of Shiraz!"

The Crusader grinned. "Now may the good Lord bless the thirsty throat of Hajji! He himself has emptied these jugs as clean as any housewife might wish. A few lees at the very bottom—just enough to cool the soles of your pretty feet. In you go!"

With both hands he caught her slim waist and lifted her, depositing her inside the big-bellied jar. Her face peered up, white and strained, as she made herself small.

"But—you?" she whispered. "Where can you go?"

"Into the jar fastened to the opposite side of the pack saddle. Now be quiet, and do not stir or speak until you see my face again!"

With that he replaced the cover, fitting it down tight, and then ran around to the left side, where a similar urn stood as balancing ballast. This jar was half filled with red wine, and as John of Lincoln felt it creep around his legs and loins, he thought wryly, Never has a man taken a queerer bath, at a more dangerous moment!

He fitted the cover down over his head, and then all was silence and blackness.

For three hours, as fat Hajji called down the wrath of Allah about his ears, Ramid ibn-Ghazi searched the caravan. The only faces he saw were those of True Believers, black with rage, or the flirtatious features of smooth-skinned women who delighted in having his handsome face thrust so close to theirs.

At last the Emir mounted his men and watched the caravan camels lurch to their feet; watched them crawl outward from the stopping place, their palanquins swaying and bobbing, the voices of their drivers calling out, "Yah yahdah! Yah yahdah!" in the ancient fashion of all cameleers.

There would be cool, sweet water ahead in the wells at Rutba, Ramid knew. There he could fill the kirbas dangling at the pommels of his men's saddles. There he could rest his thousand horses for the long wayfaring that would take them on to Baghdad.

"Somehow they hid themselves! Or else they left the caravan and went on alone," he whispered in his teeth.

"But they'll be ahead, riding to Samarkand. I'll find them if I have to go over every inch of ground between here and there!"

Ramid ibn-Ghazi stood in his stirrups and waved his Mamelukes forward. They went past the slow caravan at a galloping pace that shook the ground.

Even in his wine jar, John of Lincoln could feel the vibrations of those four thousand hoofs. He guessed what caused them and grinned at thought of the rage that must be eating the Emir.

When that furious drumming had faded into silence, and when the lurching of the wine jar grew too much to take, the Crusader lifted the cover and gulped the hot desert air. Then he raised himself from the jug and dropped to the ground, calling out to Hajji, who rode a swift Bactrian dromedary.

The fat man felt his eyes bulge at sight of the wine-wet Crusader. "Now may Allah keep me always in the shadow of His friendship! Where were you? Even while I cursed that fool of an emir, I wondered if you might be a sorcerer, to become invisible at will!"

"No sorcerer, and no thief either, though I used a thief's trick!" He went on to tell the *bashi* of the wine jars and the burden they carried. "I'll pay you for the wine my dusty boots spoiled, and bless you for the wit that made you keep a still tongue in your head."

Hajji grinned. "No pay is needed, though I'll accept your blessings, being a sinful man. There is a different sort of wine awaiting me at Rutba. The wine of Isfahan, fragrant and rich. I keep it there against the last half of my journey. Tell me again, unbeliever, how you fooled Ramid."

As he drew Shirzade from her jug, he related again his little ruse. Hajji's cackles of delight brought the sour-faced merchants forward, and now John of Lincoln had to relate again and again how the idea occurred to him, and how he felt inside the dark, wet jar. The circle of grinning faces made the Crusader realize that he had made himself a host of eager friends.

The women took Shirzade with them, to wash and brush down her clothes. The traders insisted that John of Lincoln share their food and waterskins.

"You will need food and drink alone on the desert," said a dealer in spikenard and incense, "for you must leave the *kafila* before Rutba wells. There are tongues that will be oiled in cordials at the caravanserai, and sooner or later that emir will learn ᐧif you are still with us."

"Ai," agreed a lean jewel seller. "I myself will give you a baggage camel to carry water and meat. I have an extra one, and it is a cheap price to pay to see a *khawand* humbled."

There was sense in the advice they gave him. Ramid ibn-Ghazi, he was assured, would need to rest his thousand horses. He would be waiting in Rutba, or at the fort at Iraki. Someone might be careless, and let slip word of how he had been fooled. John of Lincoln would receive no second chance so to trick the Emir. He must depart at once.

Side by side, with reins in their hands and a dromedary fitted with waterskins and panniers of food behind them, John and Shirzade stood and watched the caravan move on across the rocky ground toward Rutba. Sadness lay in them, for they had made good friends and had found happiness in each other on that caravan. And so they stood and watched it sway out of their lives, and knew that they were putting something infinitely precious behind them.

Ahmed the Assassin rode a fine gray gelding, with his lean thighs straddling a black leather saddle of Aleppo craftsmanship. The big green emerald that the Lady Hodierna had pressed into his hand to defray any added expenses he might encounter grew larger and more valuable at every mile, for he rode across the endless wastes of these limestone plateaus as guest of the Seljuk war lord Imadeddin Zengi, and what expenses did a man incur whose food and wine were free, as was the horse that rocked along so steadily under him? Thus Ahmed knew satisfaction, and dreamed away the miles with visions of the houri who had brightened his last visit to Alamut.

It was with no haste in him that he sat in his black saddle and watched the Seljuks examine caravan after caravan that went by the courier road from Damascus to Kubaisa. Imadeddin Zengi wanted some woman, a princess from Samarkand. He wanted a man who fled along this same path. Once the Seljuk found the woman, he would find the man. Meanwhile, the Seljuks did the work and Ahmed watched.

The Seljuks moved like a dark wind on to the wells at Melossa, and then eastward toward Muheiwir. No caravan held those they sought, but more than once the Ismailite heard Imadeddin Zengi swear by the steed of Allah, the fabled Burak, that he would go on to far Cathay if he must to lay hands on the ivory woman.

Ahmed was a patient man. He would only smile and nod, and tighten his brown fingers about the haft of his killing knife.

There were vast mud flats east of Rutba wells. The sun baked and dried them, and they left no track of hoof or pad as John of Lincoln and the Princess Shirzade galloped steadily across the endless miles. They crossed a finger of a rocky tableland the paynims called el-Hamad, and traversed a fringe of the Wadi Hauran, riding over hard, volcanic lands pitted with the dead stone cones of ancient geysers.

John of Lincoln was baked brown and lean by the desert sun, until he came to look the part of the infidel that he played. The Princess Shirzade, more used to these lands, retained her pallor of smooth ivory, though her *tschim* and *salta* were rimed with dust and the stains of travel.

Once they took shelter from a blistering sandstorm that came sweeping out of the north as though driven by howling jinn. With their heads lowered into the gale that stung with tiny sand bullets, their barracan hoods filtering the hot air for laboring lungs, they clung hip to thigh, clasped hands giving needed assurance to numbed bodies.

They rode past ancient ruins towering lonely and desolate on these barren wastes. They dug water from wells that had not felt the touch of man in uncounted centuries. Sitting cross-legged at dusk, they ate sparingly of meat and bread, or chewed on the Malban figs and Jerusalem raisins that had been the gift of the caravan traders.

For a week they lived their nomad life, and found it an added bond between them. Their love was being welded by the desert sun and the fury of the wind into a fierce, living flame.

They came to the banks of the muddy Euphrates during the middle of a day, and walked their horses under shading poplar trees. They crossed the river at a shallow ford below al-Anbar and galloped swiftly along the stone copings of the great Nahr Isa canal until darkness overtook them, a little over a dozen miles from the minarets of Baghdad.

The morning was well advanced next day when they came clattering through the high-arched Gate of Travelers to move through twisting narrow streets filled with shopkeepers selling brocades from Fasa and Chinese porcelains, Tawwaj carpets and sugar sticks. There was a thriving life in the Round City, for her miles-long wharves docked ships from the Malabar coast and Malaya, from Africa and Ceylon. River craft anchored offshore until the *sûk* merchants sent their slaves to unload furs and raw silks, velvets and ceramic wares, turquoise from Afghanistan and Arabic incense.

John of Lincoln and Shirzade drank in this teeming metropolis with big eyes. They walked their horses, listening to the hoarse shouts of the sellers of foodstuffs and the querulous arguments of merchants bartering jewels for golden miskals.

As they moved between a stall hung heavy with thick Persian carpets and a small shop whose counters gleamed with lapis lazuli from the Khorosan steppes, Shirzade cried out in fear.

John of Lincoln whirled.

A dozen feet away, plunging toward them even as he dragged his curving scimitar from a damascened scabbard, was the young Seljuk captain Nasran ibn-Afdal.

Chapter Twelve

T .ERE WAS NO TIME TO THINK. The Seljuk captain carried a score of men at his heels, and his shouts and cries were alerting the entire marketplace to the fact that a cursed infidel and an escaped *bayki*, who had eluded him across the *badiyah* from Damascus, were now at the length of a man's arm. Avenues opened to the Seljuk warriors through which they plunged with steel naked to the sunlight.

John of Lincoln roared once, a ringing cry that scattered men before his black stallion and the bay horse that came plunging after him. They left the camel behind them, for they had thought only for the streets that opened before their racing mounts. With heads tucked low they rode, shouting a path for pounding hoofs.

The Crusader knew that Nasran ibn-Afdal had no horse under him, and to that one fact he owed his life. He rode like a man bewitched for minutes, then reined in close to the high stone wall of the slave market.

He said, "He will find horses and come after us. Where can we hide now?"

Shirzade let bitter laughter rise from her soft red mouth. "All gates will be closed to us, for Imadeddin Zengi and his captains are much respected in Baghdad. The *muhtasib*—their chief of police—will have his men moving from *sûk* to *sûk* and house to house! We know no one here. Who will shelter a man and woman against such enemies?"

There was despair in her voice, and in the manner in which she drooped in her red leather saddle. The eyes she showed him above her dusty yashmak were wet with tears.

She whispered, "We've come so far, Yukhannan! To fail like this, within hurling distance of the great silk road to Samarkand—"

His grin challenged her. "We haven't failed! Not yet! Listen!"

They could hear the singsong call of the slave seller as it boasted the white beauty of a captured Circassan girl. The faint murmur of voices orchestrated those rising and falling tones. Men were gathered behind those walls, men who bought and sold human flesh; muscled flesh for the saltpeter mines along the Euphrates, or soft and pampered flesh for the entertainment of some bored nobleman.

As her bay mount danced uneasily under her, the Khorosan woman widened her eyes, lifting arched black brows. "The slave mart? You mean to sell ourselves as slaves?"

John of Lincoln grunted savagely, "No sane man would look there for us!"

"*Mashallah!* I'm crazy enough to agree with you!"

"What other way is there?"

However Shirzade might have answered him, John of Lincoln was never to know. For in that instant of her hesitation, they could hear the shouting voices of approaching street soldiers. The Samarkand princess was out of her saddle and slapping the rump of her bay mount. She cried out, "Then hurry, *bagatur!* If we're to seek shelter, we mustn't be seen going over those walls!"

John of Lincoln put a hand down and brought her up beside him, together with his spiked steel ball in its leathern sack. Then as Thane stood like a black rock, he rose to his full height in his worn leather saddle and lifted the Princess Shirzade to the top of the slave mart wall. With a bound he joined her and watched the black stallion trot away from him, obedient to his last command.

The great slave market of Baghdad stretched before them. Huge red silk tents were spread beside lesser canopies, and here and there gilded wooden blocks, where the slaves were offered to the buyers, thrust themselves like giant drums between the tents. To one side were the pens where Brahma bulls bellowed angrily beside pacing panthers and caged leopards, where falcons brooded sullenly, hooded and silent. Occasionally a lion would cough his resentment of the bars that penned him in, and when he did, the other animals fell silent.

In one of those moments of silence, John of Lincoln brought Shirzade down from the tall wall. Under the branches of a flowering bush he hid the sack that held his spiked ball. With it he put the clothes he wore, retaining only a strip of silk twisted about his loins in the manner of male slaves. The Khorosan princess laughed softly as she writhed out of her brocade *salta* and dusty *tschim,* to stand in transparent silk *kamis*. Then her arms flashed and the *kamis* lay in a tiny pool of white beside the *salta* and the *tschim*.

Her cheeks were red.

"It is thus they inspect the women slaves, Yukhannan. To wear clothing and yet to pose as a slave girl seeking a buyer would be to invite suspicion."

He was on the ground, lifting her clothes to her as he said, "Then put them on! I want no—"

He had no chance to finish. Beyond the wall the shouting of the seeking soldiers grew nearer, attracting the attention of the buyers and the sellers of human flesh in the great slave market.

Shirzade hissed, "Hide them, quickly! Then come, with the speed of Burak!"

He had time only to thrust her garments into the hole and scoop dirt over them; then he was running past a wooden cage filled with saluki hounds toward a massive green silk structure that Shirzade whispered was the women's quarter. Familiar with the slave marts of Samarkand and Balkh, she found her way as a wolf might find its way in its own den.

Her white hand lifted a section of the green silk, and the man could see naked women standing inside, or lolling lazily on puffy cushions: Sunnite women and Afghans, dusky girls from beyond the Pamirs and white Circassans and Georgians. Here and there his bemused eye caught the face of a plump Cathayan or the auburn hair of a lost Russ woman. Shirzade was whispering, "Over there, in the red tent—the male slaves! Be quick, for love of your Christus!" And then the green silk flap went down and shook a little in the breeze, and John of Lincoln, who was now the slave Yukhannan, went racing in great bounds toward the red silk baldachin.

He slid under the tent to find himself among men who stared at him in sullen apathy or total indifference. Most of them were men big like himself, with rolling muscles under skins the color of mahogany, or red with sun. In the shadows sat a few tall ebon savages stolen during a raid on the African coast. They knew what their fate would be, these men: the mines or the salt deserts, or hard work in some palace workroom. One out of two hundred might take the eye of a rich widow and be put to a more intimate service, then be killed with a slim *peshkab* between the ribs, lest his tongue babble of her favors.

No one stopped him when he pushed to the fore of the slave tent and stood looking out. If he wanted to catch the eye of the seller of men, why stop the fool? They eyed him for a little while, then turned away to their bitter memories.

How long John of Lincoln stood at the open tent flap, he could not guess. He watched the buyers of men and women bid for proud Turkish women and shrinking Greek girls. He saw gold coins flash in the sunlight as the bidding went high for a Bulgar with skin white as new snow. Even when he heard shouts and yells from the big green tent, he suspected nothing until he saw a woman convulsively fighting the two *khisyan* who were dragging her toward the big round selling block.

He needed no second look at that ivory skin to know her. He did not need to see the flailing whip of her long black hair as she fought savagely, bending to kick and hit, arching her back to snap with small hard teeth at wrists or fingers that came too close. He knew all that white wonder of Princess Shirzade; and he knew hot red hate for the men who cried out and laughed as she was yanked forward to the top of the great marble rostrum to stand alone and naked before their eyes.

John of Lincoln balled his fists at his hard thighs. His brain roared. If she is bought by a master and lives in far-off Mecca or Delhi, how will I ever find her again? Inside him, he was sick, knowing he had gambled that they would not be discovered, and had lost.

Yussuf al-Zayda fancied himself as a man without a vice. He chewed a sweetmeat and let his eyes move over the heaving bosom of this Khorosan woman who stood so proudly and so straight before him. Even this bit of sweet he munched, he reflected, he could do without. The woman up there meant nothing to him. Did he not, like the revered Omar ibn-Rabiyah of poetic memory, possess seventy concubines with soft hands and scented hair? But even while he congratulated himself on his virtue, Yussuf al-Zayda bethought himself that he was also chief vizier to the Caliph himself, may Allah bless his name! And the Prophet knew that al-Muktafi was no mirror of any virtue at all.

Yussuf narrowed his eyes, running them over the slim ankles and pretty legs of the ivory woman. Hai! Yussuf swallowed his sweetmeat and lurched forward, elbowing

a path between the babbling merchants and emirs who
were shouting their appreciation of such skin.

"A thousand golden dinars for the ivory one," shouted
Yussuf. Then, a little sententiously, he added, "She will
be a fine addition for the harem of our beloved caliph,
al-Muktafi! She will gladden his heart indeed."

"It won't be his heart she'll gladden," grunted a poorer
trader, knowing the fair one on the block was beyond his
reach.

Laughter rose up around the selling circle as the buyers
pressed even closer. An emir whose beard was black as
the heart of a cinder cried out through the laughter, "I
bid two thousand gold dinars for the woman! I am more
in need of having my heart gladdened than the Caliph!"

Yussuf drew himself up to his full five feet three of
rotund height. He shouted, "Twenty-five thousand gold-
en dinars! Now halt the sale and wrap her in soft silks
and woolens, that no further eyes may see the—"

Twenty-five thousand golden dinars was the ransom
of a prince of the blood. But it was not that fabulous sum,
shouted as it was in the hoarse, proud tones of Yussuf
al-Zayda, that made the emir and buyers cry out. Golden
dinars were only money. The great Brahma bull bearing
down on them with horns lowered and foam flecking his
loose, shaking lips was death itself.

Yussuf al-Zayda took one horrified look at those horns
and whirled on a toe and fled. He cursed the pride that
had made him don this morning the flowing silk *bisht*
and the wide velvet slippers and the sashed silken trousers that hid the size of his legs. These were not garments
made for running! He slipped and went to a knee.

A glance over his shoulder showed him the bull less
than ten feet away. "Allah! Praise Allah the good and the
merciful!" he screamed. "A hundred silver statues in the
prayer niches of the great mosque for my safety!"

He could hear the frenzied screams of the merchants
and the traders as they scattered. There would be no help
from them.

Yussuf al-Zayda swore from this day to the time of his
death that he felt the touch of a bull horn at his back.

In the next moment the bull was falling away from
him, swerving aside and staggering as if filled with a
hundred rotls of heady wine. By Allah! There was a
naked man clinging to his horns! Yussuf al-Zayda watched

with his breath stuck in his throat as the man brought
the huge muscles of his wide shoulders and long arms
into play, hanging by a hip and a leg to the shoulder of
the big Brahma. The naked man seemed possessed of no
fear. He hung on and his teeth showed where his lips
drew back to feed his heaving lungs with air.

Slowly the man was bending the thick neck of the bull.

The great Brahma tried to stand on wide-braced fore-
legs, but the very momentum of his charge betrayed him.
The hands that held that weight to his horns was a living
anchor slowing him, tipping him slowly off balance. The
Brahma blew lustily, shaking foam from his lips. He tried
to bellow, but his neck was being twisted far to one side,
so that all he could achieve was a feeble grunt.

The naked man had both bare feet on the ground now.
His arms were straight as they thrust down savagely. His
shoulders heaved again, and he came off his feet to get
every added pound of weight to the force he applied.

The Brahma collapsed and rolled in the dust, and now
the naked man knelt astride his thick neck until shouting
khisyan could bring ropes and sticks and lash the bull to
helplessness.

Yussuf al-Zayda drew air into his lungs. His shaking
hands he hid under the silks of his caftan. Carefully he
strode forward to face the big man whose muscles and
courage had saved his life.

"I vowed a hundred silver statues for my life," he said,
wheezing with the fear that still ran in him. "No man can
say that Yussuf al-Zayda is cheap or miserly! Should I do
less for him to whose arms Allah lent strength to accomplish His will?"

The naked man bowed his head a trifle awkwardly.
John of Lincoln was not used to a slave role, and besides,
he needed the length of his throat through which to bring
air into his sobbing lungs.

The Chief Vizier mistook his silence for humility, and
became even more affable. "By the beard of the Prophet!
If you were a eunuch, I'd reward you by purchasing you
for the royal harem, to watch over the womenfolk of my
royal master! It would be an easy life, in truth!"

John of Lincoln found his tongue then. "O Lord of
Generous Givers, your wisdom is equaled only by your
discernment. I am a eunuch, a Frankish knight emascu-
lated in revenge by a jealous emir."

Yussuf chuckled. He did not quite believe that this big Frangi lacked his manhood. No mere eunuch could have topped that bull! But Yussuf al-Zayda felt expansive, and if the man lied, the torturers of the Caliph would make him regret it, if ever he overstepped his bounds.

Yussuf whirled with regal pomp to the cowering seller of slaves. "Fool and father of fools! Your besotted stupidity threatened my life, and the lives of those other buyers of your wares! For the defective pen in which you kept this bull, I could have you hung up on sharp hooks in the city square for the birds to eat!"

The slave seller groveled. The pen that held the bull was a strong one; he himself had seen to its proper building. Still, he dared not protest, for he saw that the Chief Vizier was merely releasing his fear in his shouted words.

"Master of wisdom," the slave dealer babbled, "receive as my gift this Frangi eunuch! He shall be yours to guard your illustrious person, or serve our royal ruler if you so desire."

Yussuf al-Zayda calculated the golden dinars this slave would bring from the Caliph, and allowed himself to be persuaded to accept the gift. "Hmmph!" he snorted, intending to bully the dealer a little longer. "A poor gift, in truth. Almost a bribe! Still, I am a generous man, without a fault. I shall take your gift and ask Allah to forgive your ignorance. Clothe the woman, then, and send the sale parchments to the Hall of the Chief Vizier, that I may sign them. There will be no parchment for the male slave, of course, since he is a gift!"

. The slave dealer allowed himself the luxury of a tight smile. "There will be no sale paper for the Frank, most generous of royal servants!"

Yussuf al-Zayda beckoned John of Lincoln to him. His eyes were sly as he whispered, "I could test your claim to eunuchhood with a plump little Georgian beauty I own, of course. But I will not. I give favors, and I expect favors in return. Do we understand each other?"

The Crusader bowed his head.

Yussuf grunted, "Good, good! There are times when a friendly hand in the royal harem can prove most useful to a chief vizier! When we get to know each other better, I will permit you to show your gratitude to me. Meanwhile, follow my retinue to the palace. Stay close beside me, for I shall take you, with the Khorosan woman, to show you to the Caliph."

John of Lincoln nodded once again. As he watched the Princess Shirzade, garbed now in silk garments that hid her from her bare feet to the fall of her black hair, his right hand held tight to the twisted muslin at his loins. There was a hard length of wood there, the pin of the pen that had held the Brahma bull.

As he followed the little retinue of the Chief Vizier, he wondered just what it was that his joust with chance had won him.

Watching them go was the slave dealer, proud and erect, now that Yussuf al-Zayda was passing out of sight beyond the stone latticework that shaded the gate of the slave mart. A frown lay on his bronzed face, for there were some aspects of this recent deal that bothered him.

He knew his slaves as he knew the faces of his concubines. The ivory woman and the Frankish knight were no slaves of his! Never before today had he seen either of them. But if Allah in His wisdom sent him a man and a woman worth twenty-five thousand golden dinars and the friendship of the Chief Vizier, should he prove a reluctant taker?

And so it was that when Nasran ibn-Afdal came storming into the slave mart seeking his prey, he was met with a blank stare and shrugging shoulders.

The slave dealer told the Seljuk captain, "Are they crazed with opium that they should seek shelter on my slave blocks? Look elsewhere for this man and woman!"

It was common sense he spoke. The Seljuk knew the men of Baghdad had no great love for him and his kind, and so he went fuming out the latticework gate as empty-handed as he had entered it, telling himself that were he the war lord Imadeddin Zengi, he would teach manners and respect to these insufferable merchants.

Nasran ibn-Afdal left behind him a contented man. The slave dealer grinned and chuckled as he wrote out the sale parchment for the Khorosan slave. A profit, a friendship won, and a chance to beard a hated Seljuk, all in the same afternoon! He felt so good that he began to contemplate taking home the Russ slave, whose red hair so fascinated all True Believers.

The scrape of his quill pen alternated with his chuckles and his anticipation of the coming night.

The palace of the Caliph of Baghdad was a wonderland of white marble and snowy alabaster, sandalwood latticework, and tiles painted red and yellow, green and purple. Gold glittered from rounded minarets and bulbous domes, from grilled windows and trefoil arches. The palace occupied a stretch of ground close by the Golden Gate and the Hall with its metal tree, whose branches were alternate limbs of solid gold and silver.

The retinue of slaves that followed Yussuf al-Zayda under the multifoil arches of the Gate of Felicity and through the inner court, between arched runways and walls of flowered tiles, formed a small part of the vast army of eunuchs and servants, slaves and soldiers who went rushing between the great confectionary kitchens and the stables, the royal chambers and the gardens.

The office of the Chief Vizier lay between the Hall of the Treasury and the Garden Kiosk. It was here that the Chief Vizier clapped his hands and sent a pair of Nubian pages with the Princess Shirzade to the Hall of the Royal Bedchamber, there to be cleaned with rose water and sprinkled with musk and perfumes for her meeting with the Caliph.

John of Lincoln was assigned to the Quarters of the Harem Slaves. He was given colored silks to don, and the necklet that was the symbol of his station in the palace. Then he was led up through tiled corridors flanked by panels that were thick with Kufic inscriptions in golden veins, scrolled with silver. There were wall fountains here, in the shapes of dolphins and fishes, spouting crystal streams of water into tanks lined with Raiy glassware. Ahead lay the royal throne room.

Al-Muktafi was caliph of Baghdad in this Moslem year 536. He was a man of middle size, with a hook nose and a black beard trimmed and scented. He sat on the cushions of the throne *diwan* from which four pillars of solid gold rose to support a brocaded canopy fringed in pearl beadings. His fleshy lips proclaimed the desires that ate at him eternally, desires that made his eyes glow as he surveyed the Princess Shirzade.

She came to him with her small ivory feet bare, their toes dyed a blood red. Her glossy black hair was done up in a net of fine golden threads, and golden anklets and *asawir* clanked musically at her every stride.

John of Lincoln had never seen the Khorosan woman

decked out as a harem concubine. He felt the blood pound
in his veins as his eyes ran from her rose face veil to her
red fingertips. Her long and shapely legs gleamed beneath
transparent rose silk.

That the caliph felt something of this allure was evidenced by the fact that he leaned forward silently, breathing through his open mouth. His eyes moved up and
down and sideways, and as he looked, he sighed softly.

"Yussuf al-Zayda, you are a robber and a thief!"

The Chief Vizier paled and trembled, bowing low. He
cried out softly, "Lord of All Wisdom! Eternal Bestower
of Riches and Delights! If I have failed in my duties, my
life is in your palm!"

Al-Muktafi laughed and slapped his knee. "Failed me,
Yussuf? You have brought me the price of a thousand
palaces! You robbed and cheated the poor slave dealer
from whom you stole this living treasure! You paid
twenty-five thousand golden dinars only? I insist you take
fifty thousand in payment for her!"

Yussuf al-Zayda cried out his delight, bobbing his head
up and down. He would have gone on in his fulsome
praise until sundown, but for the waving hand of his
caliph.

"Bring the woman to me in the hour of dusk, Yussuf.
I will receive her in the royal bedchamber."

The Caliph brought his fine, dark eyes around to the
figure of the Crusader. "And the man?"

Yussuf al-Zayda babbled of the manner in which the
Frank eunuch had thrown the big Brahma bull at the
moment when he, Yussuf al-Zayda, felt its horn touching
his very back. "I promised him a task for life, Bestower of
All Blessings. A station at the gate of the royal harem, that
he might grow fat and plump reflecting on the generosity
of the caliph of all caliphs."

"It shall be done, Yussuf. To have lost you, whose eye
for beauty is almost as discerning as my own, would have
been unthinkable. Give him every privilege. Let him
guard the loveliness of my concubines as he guarded your
life!"

The royal door of the harem was a masterpiece of the
Moresque arch, inlaid with mother-of-pearl and lapis
lazuli, its columns of black marble veined in green. From
its red sill the harem floor of checkered black and white

tile stretched away toward distant latticed windows. A
row of slender columns gave added depth to the vast
chamber, in which a fountain of tiled marble splashed
scented waters as the hub of a great pool.

Women were bathing in that pool as the Chief Vizier
stationed John of Lincoln at the doorway. He carried a
great, two-handed scimitar and his wide black trousers
were belted with red leather. On his feet he wore match-
ing slippers. His chest was naked, but thin armbands of
gold were fastened about his thick wrists. He looked more
the virile fighting man than he did a harem eunuch, and
the wondering glances of the concubines roved his bulk
with something of challenge mixed with their curiosity.

The big Crusader stood embarrassed at the doorway,
scimitar grounded between his feet. He tried not to hear
the laughter and the chatter of the concubines, tried not
to notice the languorous glances they threw his way. Some
of them crawled from the sheltering waters of the pool
and paraded around its tiled rim, water dripping from
them. They teased him with their mocking laughter and
their posturings.

It took all the will power he could command to fasten
his eyes on the great bronze lamp that hung from the
groined ceiling on heavy brass chains, and glue them
there. He tried to close his ears to their voices and blind
his eyes to their flesh.

John of Lincoln was congratulating himself on his im-
perturbability when he felt a cool wet hand touch his ribs.

A mocking voice whispered, almost in his ear, "You are
no eunuch, man with the white skin! I can feel your heart
thudding like a water pump under my palm!"

With his eyes studying the hanging lamp, John of Lincoln said, "I have been running, lady of the harem."

A tickling finger touched the corner of his lips. "Liar!
No man can fool Shamsiyah, the daughter of the Nile!
Your blood runs like molten metal at sight of us. You
dare not look down at me!"

The room was suddenly silent, and as the Crusader let
his gaze drop from the lamp to the length of the great
chamber, he saw that it stood empty, except for the
woman at his side and the shadows that grew longer on
the black and white floor. It was nearing dusk beyond the
arched windows. Faintly he could hear the cry of a muez-
zin from the slim minaret beyond the horse fountain. The

bathing women were gone, the little wet prints of their feet still glistening on the tile floor.

The Egyptian woman sighed and murmured, "There are no eyes to see you now, Frangi. I am no Persian harlot, to betray you to the Chief Vizier. Look at me!"

The thought came to John of Lincoln that it might be well to win himself a friend in the harem, even such a friend as this amorous Egyptian. If ever he was to escape the tiled walls and colonnades of the caliphal palace, he would need other hands than his own to open barred doors.

His voice was hoarse as he whispered, "You are a royal concubine. If I were to let my eyes look at you, my head would roll from my shoulders by dawn."

"Shamsiyah is no concubine! I am the ninth wife of al-Muktafi! Wedded as a matter of state policy, and ignored by him ever since the night of my wedding, five years ago!"

Two wet arms crept around his neck. He could not help seeing the dusky face that was so close to his own. Her eyes were black and limpid, their lids darkened blue with kohl, her mouth red and big, soft with the hunger that ate in her. Thick black hair was draped like a wet shawl halfway down her lissom back.

Shamsiyah whispered, "Take away that sword blade, *nasrany!*".

He slipped the scimitar aside, and in that moment the Egyptian threw her arms about him. She gurgled laughter through the lips that sought his mouth.

"Father of liars! Prince of falsehoods! You are no eunuch!"

For a maddening moment, her lips pressed against his, and then she was writhing free and running, a slim brown shape in the darkening shadows, trailing laughter behind her.

It was a badly shaken Crusader who stood like a graven statue, staring into the shadows where she had disappeared. He was alone now, for the first time since he had trailed the Chief Vizier into the palace. Somewhere in this colossal marble pile was Shirzade. Somehow he had to reach her, to defend her from the Caliph, who had summoned her to be brought to him at the hour of dusk. Through the windows beyond the pool, that dusk was even now seeping onto the palace grounds.

He whirled on a heel to begin his search.

A footfall brought him to a halt.

The lamplighter came moving into the darkening room, lifting his long wooden pole to touch the flame at its metal end to the hanging lamp. As radiance flooded this part of the chamber, John of Lincoln saw that the man, a brown-skinned Afghan, was scowling heavily.

The Crusader said, "You sigh like a man whose best friend was hung up on metalhooks for the birds to eat!"

"Your jest almost hits the mark, Frank," said the lamplighter, grounding his pole to lean on its haft with clasped hands. "Within the past hour the Caliph has sent three slaves to the torture dungeons beneath the Gate of the Dead. He is in a royal rage. Nobody dares go near him."

John of Lincoln grunted. "Did he hurt his little toe? Or weren't the sweetmeats sugared enough to suit his taste?"

The Afghan grinned. "Nothing as forgivable as that, by Allah! He lives only for his women, this al-Muktafi. I understand some Khorosan beauty the Chief Vizier bought today in the slave mart will not be able to bed with him this night."

John of Lincoln felt his heart grow cold in his chest. He took two steps forward and caught the lamplighter by an arm, half lifting him into the air with the fury of his emotion.

"This Khorosan! What happened to her? Did she kill herself? Did—"

"By the camels the Prophet drove to Mecca, release me!"

"I'll release you when you tell me what I want to know!"

The Afghan sighed, reading the rage that was in the eyes of this mad Frank. "Has the world gone crazy tonight? The Caliph sends his favorites to the torture chambers, and now a *nasrany* guard threatens to tear my arm off at the shoulder! The Khorosan is safe enough, by Allah. It's just the moon sickness that has come upon her. Now will you let me go?"

John of Lincoln relaxed and let his arm fall. A smile twisted his mouth. He said, "My apologies, man from the south. I was bought at the same time as the Khorosan. I conceived an interest in her welfare. She's a pretty thing."

The Afghan chuckled. "A eunuch—with an interest in

a woman? Ah, well! Perhaps the day of miracles isn't over yet." His bright black eyes peered through the shadows. "It might be that we'll be friends, we two. I've an interest myself in a little Circassan that Yussuf bought two years back. Al-Muktafi enjoys them once, then forgets them. Somebody has to keep the little darlings happy!"

The lamplighter moved on, brightening the chamber as he went, leaving John of Lincoln brooding over his great scimitar, wondering where in this palace acreage the Princess Shirzade might be, and if despair troubled her slumbers as it did his thoughts.

Ahmed the Ismailite moved through the *sûk* of the rug sellers, his alert eyes questing from the high wooden racks where hung the woven masterpieces of Nisapur and Shustar to the dark, bearded faces of the men who sold them. Less than an hour before dawn he had ridden into Baghdad from the Seljuk encampment along the banks of the Tigris. Ahmed trusted no man to track down his quarry. With his own eyes and lips he would seek and find the Crusader.

Ahmed walked with a sense of haste strong within him. He had been in earshot when the young captain Nasran ibn-Afdal made his report to Imadeddin Zengi. He had seen the towering rage into which that report had flung the Seljuk war lord. Twice had the young captain had the woman Imadeddin Zengi sought within reach of his hands. Twice he had failed. The third time would mean his neck.

Listening to Imadeddin Zengi make that threat, the Assassin had smiled. He smiled again now, contemptuously, as he pushed through the crowded *sûk*. The fool trusts to his own senses, he thought. I use the senses of other men to find what I seek.

The Assassin paused to engage a pearl seller in idle talk, praising his rosy wares and lamenting the flatness of his purse that would not permit him to purchase one of the glistening balls. From the pearl seller he learned the details of the chase that had taken place within a dozen feet of the little stall. But when he asked if a Crusader knight was within Baghdad's walls, a big man with yellow hair and a spiked ball, the pearl seller looked incredulous.

"Where in Baghdad would an infidel find haven?" he demanded.

It was a question Ahmed had asked himself more than once. He had counted on the fact to put him within dagger reach of the Crusader once he reached the Round City. Ahmed moved on, telling himself that there were other sellers, all along the street. One of them would have seen the big Crusader. It was with confidence that he headed toward a tall Tibriz man who sold cinnamon in tiny copper jars.

Chapter Thirteen

THE HAREM gardens lay west of the Mosque of the Black Pearl. They were approached by a wide marble stair, flanked by rows of flowering shrubs. Here on colored flaggings, between low sandalwood benches and marble arbors, the women of the harem sat and talked, or strolled together down the wide walks. Only Shamsiyah the Egyptian did not walk or sit with the others. Her dark, slanted eyes were aimed at the new Christian slave.

The ninth wife of al-Muktafi was bored with life. For too long she had sighed in these gardens, or stared upward at a mellow moon as her shoulder traced the imprint of an ivory column, lonely and ignored. The blood that flushed her skin to its dusky copper tint was too warm to allow such indifference to continue.

Shamsiyah sighed, noting the breadth of the Christian's shoulders, and the muscles of his long arms. A delicate shiver made her glance to left and right, to see if she were observed. The thought of nestling her cheek against those shoulders while those powerful arms squeezed her into submission was overpowering. Seeing that no eyes were on her, the Egyptian rose to her feet and moved stealthily toward John of Lincoln.

Shamsiyah pretended interest in the rosebushes that thrust their big scarlet blooms against the spokes of a low marble railing. But she so contrived her posture that her whispers would carry to the ears of the big Crusader.

"I have not seen you in the room of the harem pool the last two days," she told him, leaning to sniff the fragrance of a flower.

"I stationed myself outside the door. It seemed the wiser thing to do."

Her full red mouth twisted into a smile. "Are you afraid of betraying the fact that you are no eunuch, Frangi?"

"Something like that."

"Coward! I waited for you. I wanted to see you again."

"I am here."

Shamsiyah hissed at him. "You know what I mean, Frank! Didn't I explain myself the other evening? I'm tired of being so much alone, left so often with only women all around me! I want the company of a man!"

Her brown hand came out and touched his arm, caressing it from the elbow to the round of his shoulder. He could not check the indrawn breath that betrayed his reaction to the Egyptian.

Her laughter seemed as fragrant as the blossoms all around them. "Haven't you realized yet that I could betray you to the Caliph?" she asked, moving her hand across his wide chest.

"What do you want with me, Shamsiyah?" he choked.

"Friendship. Affection. Escape." As his eyes slued around to her, she let him read the determination in her soft brown eyes. "I said escape. Escape from this place where no one cares what happens to Shamsiyah, daughter of Pharaohs!"

Escape! The word was a tocsin bell that sent the blood of the Crusader thudding in his veins. Escape, now—before the moon sickness left the Princess Shirzade! Before the amorous al-Muktafi summoned her to share the wide cushioned bed of the royal bedchamber! With this thought in mind, John of Lincoln set himself to win over the neglected Egyptian.

His first act in this new role was to hook her slim waist with an arm and bring her down a narrow winding path between high hedges. It was not a difficult task he gave himself, he admitted, for the skin of this slim brown woman was as smooth as Tus velvet, and as hot as the desert simoom. When they were secluded behind the broad fronds of a flowering bush, she allowed him to draw her close, her hands warm on his back.

She whispered between kisses, "We can go away from Baghdad together, Frangi. They have forgotten the existence of Shamsiyah at the palace. I have kept to myself since my arrival. I speak only to a few of the wives, and to al-Muktafi's concubines not at all. Nobody would miss me, until it would be too late!"

"How could we do it?" he asked.

"Two swift horses. Horses from Oman. With food bags and waterskins tied to the saddles. At the hour of midnight, when the palace sleeps and even the guards nod in slumber, we could meet at the mounting block beyond the Fountain Gate."

Arab horses, food, and water! This was an offer heady enough to make the Crusader tremble. Shamsiyah felt his shiver, and smiled dreamily to herself as she rested her face against his chest. She whispered, "You know the Holy Land. You could guide us back to Cairo. My father is wealthy. He will reward you well, when I tell him to do so. Of course, marriage between us is forbidden by the Koran, but there is no law that says I cannot have you always near me, as the master of my household." Shamsiyah laughed softly. "That will be an even better occupation than this. Me, and your freedom!"

They strolled a little farther along the path, the Egyptian a few paces to the fore, the Crusader picking the flowers at which she pointed. In the closeness this task imposed on them, Shamsiyah whispered final directions.

"We will go tonight," she told him, "at the hour of midnight! Remember, meet me at the mounting block beyond the Fountain Gate. I will be there, clad in *chalwar* and caftan, looking like a man. I will secure a royal signet that will pass us out of the palace. Frank, on your life, do not fail me!"

He wondered at her haste to be gone. For five years she had waited here in this palace for this moment, and now that it was come, she was reaching for it with greedy fingers. It was on the tip of his tongue to ask her to wait—for he would need time to alert Shirzade—but as they rounded a bend in the path, two concubines came walking toward them.

Shamsiyah reached for the flowers John of Lincoln had picked at her request. With her face buried in their fragrant blooms, she passed the approaching women without a glance.

John of Lincoln swung on a heel and moved as fast as discretion would allow toward the marble stair. From these steps to the Corridor of Armed Slaves was only fifty feet, and from there to the sandalwood door of the harem quarter was only another hundred. The Princess Shirzade would be behind that carved door, somewhere in the chambers allotted to the harem women.

A black guard grounded his lance as the Crusader approached.

John of Lincoln said, "I come to see the new Khorosan slave woman purchased by Yussaf al-Zayda."

"Wait," the Somalilander directed him.

The lancer returned with a fat woman whose title was the Mother of Female Slaves. Her piercing black eyes studied the Crusader with honest suspicion. "What brings a palace eunuch to see the most recent bride to be of our glorious master?"

John of Lincoln salaamed low. "Word from Shamsiyah the Egyptian, ninth wife of the glorious al-Muktafi. She sends words of felicitation. I am to speak these words only into the ears of the Khorosan woman."

The Mother of Female Slaves sniffed audibly. "The Egyptian is as much a fool as she is a dreamer! Her and her hoity-toity airs! Who does she think she is? You go back and tell her that you interrupted me in the midst of stitching the twenty silken veils on the Persian woman. Veils the wise and righteous caliph will tear from her this very evening."

"This evening?"

John of Lincoln was aware that he gaped stupidly, like a witless clod, but the sheer shock of this news drove all reason from him. Tonight!

He realized now why Shamsiyah had chosen this night to flee the palace. Al-Muktafi would be so concerned with those twenty silken veils and what lay under them that there would be little heed paid to the palace retinue. Wines would pour like the water of a cascade. Men would be sodden in drink by midnight, celebrating the wedding of the caliph. And John of Lincoln would be riding hard beside a fleeing wife, leaving the Princess Shirzade behind!

There was no sorrow left in Shirzade of Samarkand. For four nights and five days she had reddened her eyes with her tears, but there comes a moment, even to a woman in love, when fate presses down its circumstances like the suffocating pillow of an executioner. Since that day in the throne room she had not seen John of Lincoln, and she dared not ask for him lest her curiosity bring him injury. Her moon sickness she welcomed, as she would any excuse to postpone the inevitable.

Now, with the Mother of Female Slaves lifting a gauzy transparency to drape it over her, Shirzade knew despair.

"The rose beneath the lemon, I think," babbled the fat woman, tilting her head to one side. "The black for very last, since al-Muktafi has a weakness for ebony and ivory. Ah, my dear! How lucky you are! Every last slave is whispering your name, for the Caliph has ordered a hundred extra skins of wine to be broken open this night, that all may drink your favor."

An orange veil floated over her shoulders as the Princess Shirzade stood like a statue. She did not feel the pudgy fingers of the Mother of Female Slaves as they adjusted the veils to suit her fancy. She had no thought save for her big Crusader, and what he might be doing at that moment.

As the fat woman turned away, Shirzade stared down at a large, jade-headed draping pin. Its blade was almost a foot long, thin and sharp as a needle. The Khorosan moved like a cat. She reached down and her hand snatched up the pin. She could not hide it among the drapes, for these would be removed, to be donned in sequence when the Caliph sent for her that evening.

With desperation spurring her glance, Shirzade gasped. The vase of cut tulips, by the latticework! None would think to look there for an errant draping pin.

And later, tonight, she told herself as she thrust the thin needle of steel deep into the water, none will think to search me for it, either.

They would not search her until too late, not until after she had plunged it deep in her heart, the heart that belonged to John of Lincoln.

A thousand torches made fiery eyes in the night as John of Lincoln moved past the Tower of the Skull toward the Mosque of the Royal Ancestors. There was an urgency in him, an urgency that made him blind to the wineskins waved in his face, that made him deaf to the shouts of the slaves and soldiers sprawling in the shadows, gulping at wine that gleamed like molten rubies where the torchlight caught it.

Somewhere beyond him, within the tiled walls of the Royal Bedchamber, the Princess Shirzade would be taken to the cushioned *diwan* of the Caliph. Unless he reached her before al-Muktafi took her in his arms, there would be no chance for them to slip out of the palace grounds and into the narrow streets of Baghdad this night.

Wryly he told himself, Even if I do reach her before the Caliph, that royal goat will have the guardsmen around my ears before I can get to the mounting block! To add despair to his hopelessness, he reflected that even were he, by some miracle, to win safety past al-Muktafi with Shirzade, it would be a bitter Shamsiyah that would be waiting at the mounting block with her Arabian horses. The

Egyptian woman would be in no mood to see him ride off with Shirzade instead of herself.

Knowing all those odds, realizing the ridiculous figure he made, striding alone against the empire of the Abbasids, John of Lincoln went on, past the bleary-eyed lancer at the gate of the Corridor of Eunuchs, and up the stairs that would take him to the ivory door that barred his ingress to the royal apartment.

The big Mameluke who stood with his ax grounded on the checkered tile of the bedchamber anteroom straightened when he saw John of Lincoln. The ax came up into his hands, and he moved forward, ax high, growling, "Harem slave, what are you doing so far from your post?"

John of Lincoln grinned stupidly. Here and there, as he crossed the courtyard below, the lees of a few wineskins had spilled their contents across his chest and legs. Now he staggered, and saw the suspicion of the Mameluke fade into amusement.

The Crusader grinned foolishly. "I came to thank the Caliph for the wine that made me drunk. Thank him and the girl he's marrying. Must be a nice girl for him to open so many wineskins!"

The guard agreed, dropping his ax to catch this harem slave by the shoulder and turn him back toward the Corridor of Eunuchs. "She is, and she knows how grateful you must be," he grunted. "But unless you want to have the skin flayed off your soles and then be made to run a hundred feet, to teach you not to walk where—*uuuff!*"

The Mameluke had never heard of England. He had never seen men use fists to fight. And so he was totally unprepared when this harem slave brought his knuckles thudding down atop his jaw. The guard felt his yell gurgle in his throat as his knees crumpled into the black pit that opened at his feet.

John of Lincoln tied the man with his own belt, and left him sprawled and gagged in the shadows. Then he was thrusting open the ivory grilled door and moving soundlessly on bare feet across the bedchamber tiles toward the wide *diwan* where a hundred cushions made a garden of reds and greens and yellows and blues and purples for the royal body this night.

What can shelter a caliph can also shelter me, the Crusader thought, and crawled clumsily under the cushions.

He had only a few minutes to wait.

The Princess Shirzade came first, clad in twenty veils as thin as a mist off the Lincolnshire marshes, with the Mother of Female Slaves at her heels. He caught the ivory wonder of her skin, gleaming through the rainbow hues. Her feet were dyed red, as were her fingertips, and her glossy black hair had been done up in a towering coiffure through which ropes of pearls had been hung. A single red ruby was hung on a golden fillet, after the Ulayyah fashion, in the middle of her forehead.

She was barbaric and lovely, with golden *khalkhals* on her ankles and bracelets making metallic music on her wrists. Her slant eyes were dark with kohl, and antimony made her eyelids glisten with blue fire.

Shirzade came with incense burning from the golden censers in the hands of the slave boys, with women scattering rose petals at her red feet, with singing girls chanting softly. She was seated on the *diwan* cushions by the Slave Mother, who arranged her veils about her, standing back to nod her head at their effect.

"You will bring blessings on our house, woman of Samarkand," the fat woman said. "You will steal the wits of al-Muktafi, and—if you have any sense about you at all—you'll be queen of the harem before the month of fasting is upon us!"

They left her alone after a while, with the incense and the rose fragrance in the air, and the departing footfalls fading out.

Soon now the Caliph would come from his feasting tables, eager to sate one kind of hunger as he had been to sate another. Shirzade brought the thin draping pin from the twist of green veil that had been its hiding place. Just once she glanced down at its needle-like length, then lifted it to drive it between her breasts.

Beside her the cushions erupted as a man sprang out. His hand came forward and closed on her wrist. The jade draping pin fell from her nerveless fingers as she sat frozen on the cushions, staring with wide, unbelieving eyes at the face of the Crusader, who appeared like a jinn from a water bottle.

"Yukhannan!" she whispered, unbelieving.

She was clad as a royal bride, in thin silks and jewels. Her eyes were slant and exotic in their blued lids and long black lashes, and the ruby on her forehead was a glob of red flame. Never before had Shirzade of Samar-

kand seemed so intoxicating to John of Lincoln as she did
in this moment, when he knelt beside her on the royal
cushions, with her fragrance a song that stirred his blood
to a mad pulsing.

He knew that al-Muktafi would be coming soon. Even
now, he might hear his footfall if he listened carefully.

Instead of listening, he put out his arms to pull his
woman in against his chest. Instead of fleeing, he knelt
there, with his mouth feeding on her lips. Gone forever
was the cold Crusader. He was elemental, almost savage
as he strained her against him as if to brand his body
with her flesh.

Shirzade whispered against his ear, "*Bagatur! Bagatur!*
We have no time for this! No time, no time!"

Yet even as she spoke, her arms tightened about him.

Sense came into them slowly. They drew apart, and
John of Lincoln whispered fiercely of the Arabian horses
from Oman tethered to the mounting block in the courtyard below.

"We'll have a wild Egyptian to deal with, if I know
Shamsiyah! She'll have the Caliph's signet on her finger.
We'll take that, and the horses, and head east!"

He pulled her to her bare feet, and in that moment
they heard the Caliph coming through the ivory latticework of the bedchamber gate.

Shirzade thrust the Crusader into the shadows.

"Wait there!" she whispered. "I'll bring him to your
hands!"

He watched from the shelter of a hanging drape as the
Khorosan ran to welcome the ruler of all Baghdad. He
heard her musical laughter and the delighted cry of al-
Muktafi. Feet padded on the tiled floor. Once the Caliph
cried out, "You lovely temptress! You tease me!"

It was then that Shirzade went whirling past him,
pirouetting on her red toes, her colored veils rippling
like living things from her shoulders. After her came the
Caliph, laughter bubbling in his throat, wheezing as he
reached out to her.

The Crusader moved like a Pamir panther. He came
out of the drapes and his hands were claws reaching for
the fat throat of al-Muktafi. He felt his fingers sink into
blubber and flesh, and the Caliph came back on his heels
as these hands held him as they would a child.

The Caliph of Baghdad had been a strong man once.

But years of easy living and the demands of his huge harem had robbed him of his strength. He felt himself lifted and shaken, even while his lungs worked madly for the air denied him by the fingers that squeezed his throat.

His bulging eyes took in the brawny harem slave, saw the fist that seemed like a slab of granite as it came thudding down into his face. Al-Muktafi felt his head explode into a thousand fragments, and he fell as an ox might fall before the ax.

"*Mashallah!*" breathed Shirzade, staring down at the inert ruler. "Did you kill him?"

"I only put him to sleep for a while. But never mind him! Shamsiyah is waiting at the mounting block."

Shirzade felt the bite of jealousy as she padded at the Crusader's heels. She whispered as they raced out into the empty Corridor of the Armed Slaves, "This Shamsiyah, now! What did you do to make her agree to help us get away?"

"By the Holy Wood! Will you save that breath for running?"

Shirzade ran, but her thoughts were vivid as her red feet flashed up and down. She frowned as John of Lincoln led her down the Stairs of a Hundred Steps, and opened her lips to speak again as they waited in the black shadows flung by a courtyard torch, backs pressed to the marble wall of the Pavilion of the Royal Harem.

As her eyes scanned the vacant court, she said, "Tell me, Yukhannan! Why did she agree to help us?"

"She didn't agree to help us. She thinks I'm running away with her, back to Egypt."

"*Inshallah!* Name of a thousand dogs! As soon as I turn my back, you're tramping off with some fat brown-skinned—"

"Quiet, as you love life!" he told her savagely. "We don't know how long al-Muktafi will stay quiet up above!"

Her little white hands were balled into fists that she wanted to smash into his face with every ounce of her lithe strength. To be forced to stand silent here, waiting, was sheer torture for the furious Khorosan. A bare red foot stamped once in the courtyard dust, a silent protest against the injustices of fate.

Then his hand was big and warm on her slim wrist and he was dragging her at a run across the yard toward the marble mounting block, which she could glimpse in the shadows of the Fountain Gate.

Two Arab barbs stood at the block, their reins in the hand of a slim brown man. Sacks of food and two bulging *kirbas* hung from the high saddle pommels. At sight of the running figures, the slim brown man came forward.

"Frangi, who is the woman? None but you and I must know of this!"

John of Lincoln ignored Shamsiyah to put both hands around the supple waist of Shirzade of Samarkand. One heave of his wide shoulders and she rose through the air to land in a saddle.

"*Wallahi!*" whispered the Egyptian incredulously. "Have you gone mad?"

"Not mad, Shamsiyah. You see, I love this woman. She's the Khorosan that al-Muktafi was to have wedded this night. The Caliph is upstairs with a sore jaw where I hit him, to keep him quiet so I could steal his bride."

John of Lincoln knew he had to silence this woman, but he was frozen at the thought of hitting her. Well he knew that she would have the armed slaves following them out the Fountain Gate as soon as they began to gallop. And so he spent his breath and precious time in talking, wondering what to do with her.

He said, "We fled from the Holy Land, Shamsiyah. We were sold together into slavery, here in Baghdad. I—"

"Father of harlots! Brother of pigs! Son of an infidel mother!" rasped the Egyptian, panting harshly. Her eyes were big and round, filled with hate and fury. "You can tell me this, after what I have done? When they flay the skin from your soles, I will whisper other methods of torture into the ears of al-Muktafi. Better for you if you had killed him!"

Shamsiyah was working herself into a towering frenzy. She vibrated as a reed vibrates in a high wind. In a moment she would be screaming in her scorn and anger.

John of Lincoln could never hit a woman, but no such compunction held Shirzade in its grip. Her hands went down and long ivory fingers wrapped themselves around the leather neck of her waterskin. A *kirba* is no weapon, but when it is filled with water until its sides bulge out, it makes a considerable weight. When that weight is backed by the jealous arms of a woman, the *kirba* is as effective as a battle mace.

As the waterskin came driving full against the top of her head, Shamsiyah went down as if boneless. John of Lincoln stared at her fallen figure until Shirzade whispered, "Hurry up, father of fools! Or are you going to stay there and memorize her face all night?"

The Crusader knelt and deftly removed the caliphal signet ring from the dusky finger of the unconscious Shamsiyah, where it gleamed like the fabled eye of Shaitan. Then his foot fumbled into the saddle, kicking the barb into a run. They raced out the Fountain Gate and across the second courtyard toward the Gate of Fertility. Sight of the caliphal signet opened the grilled gates. Then they were pounding through a square and down a cobblestoned alley.

"We'll make for the slave mart," John of Lincoln said, with the wind whipping his words away as fast as he spoke. "We'll get our clothes and be twenty miles away by sunup."

Shirzade of Samarkand made no answer. She rode with her thin silks almost torn from her body, with the moonlight coating her ivory skin so that she seemed a silver statue. Her alert eyes had seen the features of the Egyptian, had taken note of her slim waist and ample hips, and the manner in which her *chalwar* exposed the shapeliness of her legs. Had Shamsiyah been fat and ugly, the Khorosan princess would have been angry enough. Now she galloped with her red mouth set in thin lines, and her slant eyes gleamed angrily when she looked at the Crusader, who rode unaware of the storm brewing beside him.

John of Lincoln reined in beside the high wall of the slave mart. In a moment he was standing on his saddle, lifting himself up and over the wall.

"Take the horses to the gate," he told Shirzade, from the top of the parapet. "I'll be there with our clothes."

It was an easy task to find the little hole where he had buried his *djebba* and trousers, and the *tschim* and *salta* of Shirzade. With these garments bunched in his left hand and his spike ball in its leathern sack dangling from his right fist he ran through the shadows of the slave market toward the main gate.

He was up and over the gate, and was fitting his *djebba* around his chest, when the continued silence of Shirzade of Samarkand stole through to him.

"You are as quiet as a mouse caught at a grain bin by a cat," he told her. "Most of the danger is past by now. You can speak freely."

It was an invitation he was to regret. Shirzade of Samarkand straightened, proud and regal even in her dusty garments. Her slant eyes were pools of raging brightness. Too late, the Crusader saw her right hand coming up fast toward his face.

The slap made a loud sound in the stillness of the night. "Son and father of a thousand goats! What did you do to the Egyptian that made her so willing to run away with you? How many times did you make love to her? I saw how she looked at you, with love making her eyes go soft. The silly little fool! To give up her wifeship to a caliph to ride to Egypt with a human goat! She should know you the way I know you! As soon as her back was turned, you'd be ogling some other poor wench! Trying to persuade her to come back to Baghdad, no doubt! *Inshallah!* You must like to cross the desert!"

Shirzade gathered air into her lungs so that she could continue. John of Lincoln stood bemused, confronted for the first time by a woman in a jealous rage.

"Was she as comforting as you found me to be? Did she pillow your head on her shoulder, as I've done in the cold of the desert nights? *Wallahi!* Son of a moon-crazed mother! Brother of pigs, she called you! When next I see a pig, I'll apologize to him!"

She talked on, stamping her feet in their dirty red boots, tilting back her head the better to see his face as her words hit out at him. With her hands made into fists she stepped forward and hammered at his chest, sobbing in her fury.

The touch of those fists on him released John of Lincoln from the pall of amazement that had held him frozen. Now his big hands came up and caught at her wrists, bending her arms back and down behind her, so that he held her pressed against him.

The Crusader kissed her like that, holding her so that she could not move, washing away her words with his lips. There was laughter in his throat as he whispered, "Little sister of temptation! Daughter of delight! Did you think any woman could lure me from your side? Hai, you must love me very much, to be so jealous!"

"Jealous! I'll show you!"

His kisses drowned her lips, and in that moment a kind of madness came to John of Lincoln. He lifted and shook her until he became aware, dimly, that he must be hurting her soft flesh with his hands.

"You called me the son of a moon-crazed mother! You, who are sister to madwomen and the daughter of witless fools! You know it's you I love! Why else did I risk my neck to face the Caliph and almost break his neck? You know what he'll do to me if his men ever set hands on my body! Yet you stand here and call me names, and threaten to apologize to pigs!"

A tiny giggle made him let her go. Her mouth curved in a smile and her eyes were suddenly shy as she pressed her cheek to his chest and put her arms about him. "Tell me more, Yukhannan! Tell me again it's me you love!"

John of Lincoln looked to heaven for guidance. It came to him what fools they were to stand here beside a slave-mart gate and quarrel, when the caliphal guard was scouring the streets for them. But Shirzade of Samarkand was soft and warm, and he was young and a little feckless of fate, and so John of Lincoln learned how sweet can be the reconciliation of lovers after a quarrel.

He had to kiss her again and again, and assure her that no pillow was ever made to equal the comfort of her shoulder. His lips must caress the eyes that had gone red with tears in the palace harem.

As they clung and kissed and whispered there in the growing Baghdad dawn, neither heard the padding of slippered feet up an adjoining alley, nor saw the lean, bearded face of the man in the striped caftan.

When the man came out onto the Street of the Slave Sellers, John of Lincoln and the Princess Shirzade were already in their high saddles, toeing their barbs into a gallop. They went by him in a rush of wind and a flutter of gray barracans.

Ahmed the Assassin drew up short to stare after them, a wry smile pursing his wide, cruel mouth.

Chapter Fourteen

THE BARE FEET of the Turkestan slave girl made faint scraping sounds on the wineshop floor. The single red scarf that hid her loins went flying as she whirled, bending forward so that her thick black hair fell like a shawl before her bright eyes. Then with a shrill *"Eeayhah!"* her head went back and her back arched. She went bobbing between the big wooden tables, laughing as the bearded men threw shimmering coins flashing through the rank air at her.

One man did not throw a coin, though he was clad in chain mail bossed in silver, with a helmet and scimitar that must be worth a hundred golden dinars lying on the wet tabletop. His hand played idly with the glass stem of his goblet, and his eyes looked moodily through space.

The coppery face of the dancing girl appeared suddenly before the dreaming Ramid ibn-Ghazi, like a vision conjured up by a sandstorm devil.

Her brown palm slid under his nose. "You like my dancing, lord? A few copper coins for poor Ayesha? A silver dinar? Even yellow gold would not make me angry!"

The captain from Damascus laughed. She was a pretty thing, with her mouth crimson with salve, and antimony making her eyes glow wickedly under the dyed blue lids. Knowing his gaze was warming to her, Ayesha shook her plump copper shoulders and laughed softly at what she read in his eyes.

Ramid ibn-Ghazi lifted a handful of coins from the velvet purse at his belt. He put them on the table and spread them out with a careless hand, so that golden miskals gleamed dully beside bright silver saracenates and yellow dinars. It was a small fortune the Emir spread there, and the dancing girl knew it.

Her yellow eyes glistened behind lowered black lashes. The tip of her tongue moistened her lips. "I know a very special dance," she whispered huskily. "A dance I would never do in public. I have a little room not far from here. If Your Magnificence would care to see that dance, I will show it to you there."

Ramid smiled, revealing his fine white teeth. "You have

a pretty tongue, *yah bint*. Can it waggle news of Baghdad to me while you dance?"

"Before or after, *yah khwaja*. But never during the dance itself!"

He swept up the coins and, tilting his cupped palm, poured them into her hands. "Tell me as we walk, girl. What news in Baghdad of a Christian knight, fleeing from Imadeddin Zengi?"

Ayesha lifted her eyes from the metal pile in her palms to this handsome emir. *Inshallah!* How she would dance for him! Anything this master of golden givers wanted, he should have! She set herself to make him happy, snatching up a cloak to wrap about herself, walking close beside him so that he could feel the softness of her hip and the graze of her elbow.

"Don't we wish we knew all that story! I've a friend in the kitchen of the Mother of Female Slaves who told me in strict secrecy that there's a woman involved. A wife of the Caliph. Some even go so far as to say *two* wives!"

"*Y'Allah!*" breathed Ramid ibn-Ghazi, hurriedly revising his estimate of John of Lincoln.

Ayesha wriggled to the admiring glance the Emir bestowed upon her. "My friend tells me further that the Caliph sports a bump on his jaw the size of a roc's egg! That this mad *nasrany* stole into the royal bedchamber and hit al-Muktafi with a battle mace! Then he kidnaped his latest bride, a Persian woman from Samarkand. There was another woman connected with the affair, one of the caliphal wives. But what part she played, I don't know."

"She probably got them horses and food," the Emir mused. "Though why should she risk her neck for them?"

Ayesha giggled. "Al-Muktafi was furious with her, but she has powerful connections. Her father owns half of Cairo. It would be bad grace to punish her, so al-Muktafi is banishing her for five years. Of course, that means forever. She'll go back to the Nile and take a dozen lovers, I suppose."

Ramid ibn-Ghazi felt excitement coursing through his lean body. From Rutba wells to Baghdad, he and his men had come at the gallop. Now they were encamped across the Tigris, close by the wharf where the caliphal galley was docked, within arrow shot of the Seljuk tents of Imadeddin Zengi. Between them there was armed truce because of the prey they sought. It was understood by Ramid ibn-Ghazi, as it was understood by the Seljuk was lord, that finding the Khorosan princess and the *dair azazil* was more important than renewing old feuds.

The hate that the Emir had conceived for the big Crusader when his black stallion had shouldered his smaller Arab mare away from the Princess Shirzade on the slopes of the Jebel Keniseh had become a living demon eating in his middle. The thought that the Frank had swung him up by his neck and sent his senses swimming from a blow of his infidel fist had maddened him.

The long nights of brooding in the serais beyond Rutba wells had added to that hate and madness, until it seemed that his life was now one long thirst for vengeance. His every waking moment was dedicated to the moment when John of Lincoln would fall into his hands. Even this dancing girl at his side would be an instrument in that revenge.

As Ayesha brought him up a narrow stone stair to the upper story of a mud-brick building along the Street of Quinces, the young emir felt triumph. If this baggage could hint at what course the Crusader took, she would have earned the coins he dumped into her hands a dozen times over.

"Wait here, lord," she whispered, gesturing at a low *diwan* as she closed the wooden door behind her. "I will prepare myself for the dance in the next room."

As she let her concealing cloak slip from her shoulders, Ramid ibn-Ghazi said, "Talk to me while you adorn yourself, loveliest of bayadères. Tell me, what other gossip do you hear from your kitchenmaid?"

"Nothing that would interest Your Worship."

She smiled, slipping through a beaded curtain into her little bedroom. Her quick fingers tugged at the red scarf and cast it from her. From an earthenware pot she poured a tiny bit of fragrant balm and rubbed it into her copper skin with circling palms. She called out, as she bent to lift silver anklets fitted with tiny bells and fasten them above her bare feet, "Though I do recall her saying that the *nasrany* plans to ride on to Samarkand. Shamsiyah— that's the ninth or tenth wife I spoke of, I can't remember the exact status—told al-Muktafi that the infidel dog loves the Khorosan. She may be guessing, but a woman is perceptive about that sort of thing."

Ayesha found musk for her slim legs and the essence of

crushed roses for her arms. A brush dipped in henna colored her toes and fingers the deep red of fresh blood. Hurrying hands lifted her thick black hair, coiling it in a spiral, setting silver sticks in it. Fresh bluing for her eyelids, a dab of antimony for her eyes, and she was almost as barbaric and lovely as she imagined herself.

The Emir called out, "When did all this happen, beauty of the tulip?"

"Two nights ago, while the palace got drunk with celebration of the marriage that never took place. The *nasrany* had the luck of the black flag of the Prophet in that respect, didn't he?"

Ayesha paused to take one last, loving glance at her reflection in the little silver mirror, and in that moment she lost her client. For when she came out through the beaded curtain into the room of the *diwan,* Ramid ibn-Ghazi was gone.

The Caliph of Baghdad pouted his annoyance. He sat cross-legged on the cushions of his wide throne, under the jeweled brocade overhang suspended between four golden pillars, and scowled darkly. He tried to ignore the martial bearing of the man in the silver chain mail and gold-bossed helmet, whose head was tilted back so proudly. No man had the right to stare so directly at a descendant of the blessed Harunal-Rashid. For a wistful moment al-Muktafi wished that those days of the Abbasid glory would return while he still ruled in Baghdad. Then his dreamings were washed from his mind by the crisp voice of the man before him.

"You break promises more easily than you do maiden's heads!" said Imadeddin Zengi. "When I needed soldiers to fight the infidel, you promised me a hundred thousand skilled archers. A handful showed up before my tents! When I asked for aid against Unur of Damascus, your tongue was swollen from babbling of the swordsmen you would send. I never saw a single man!

"Now I ask for news of this Persian *bayki,* this Khorosan woman, and again I get a promise. As well scoop a palmful of air and bestow it on me!"

Al-Muktafi felt his neck grow red with the rage he dared not express. He knew only too well that the Seljuk war lord could reduce Baghdad to rubble in a week. Subduing his rage, he glossed his voice with courtesy.

"Defender of the Faith! Lion of Islam! The princess was to have been my bride. She was snatched away from my arms by a mad infidel dog who hammered my skull with a battle mace!"

Imadeddin Zengi barked scornful laughter. "If the Crusader had used a mace, your skull would have been splattered across a score of tiles! He only used his fist!"

The Caliph swallowed hard, queasy in his stomach at the mental image the words of the Seljuk war lord summoned up. He said, "The fault belongs to my ninth wife, Shamsiyah. If her father weren't so cursed wealthy, I'd have her hung by her—"

"Yes, yes," interrupted the Seljuk with a wave of his hand. "I can picture to myself what you would do. Bring this woman to me. She may give me the news I seek."

Al-Muktafi clapped his royal palms. "Bring Shamsiyah to my presence," he directed, and a slave bowed out backward.

A little silence fell upon the throne room. The Caliph was too distressed by all this wild activity of late to indulge in idle chatter. He sat and scowled at Imadeddin Zengi, who ignored him to converse in low tones with the officers that flanked him.

Shamsiyah came quickly, striding forward with purpose in her long brown legs. The word that she was being banished to her beloved Nile acted as a tonic to her boredom. Almost she could find it in her heart to forgive the infidel slave who had fled without her. Soon she would be in Egypt, no longer confined and ignored within these harem walls, but free to find love where she would.

She smiled at the Seljuk commander, eyes bold and admiring. There was no reticence in her. The fact that she was safe from punishment put an added tartness on her tongue. Shamsiyah told Imadeddin Zengi everything he wanted to know. "They will ride for Samarkand. Their horses are barbs from Oman, fast and enduring. I selected them with care, thinking I would be on one of them."

Her laughter was amused, rather than bitter. "The things a woman does these days, just to get a man! If our most gracious ruler spent more than just a bridal night with his wives, maybe they wouldn't have to look elsewhere for companionship."

Imadeddin Zengi brooded at the spirited Egyptian. He said, "Woman, I understand you have been banished. I will take no chance on al-Muktafi's breaking his word to you, as he has to me, again and again. I could never sleep nights if he put hooks through those legs or hot brands on your arms." He swung to the Caliph, who squirmed in his rage and embarrassment. "You hear me, son of a Turkish slave woman?"

Al-Muktafi shouted shrilly, "I hear you, Seljuk! And now, lest I loose the wrath that I seek, in my kindliness, to overcome, depart at once from Baghdad!"

Imadeddin Zengi bowed slightly. "I leave, and with me leaves the lady Shamsiyah."

"Take her, take her! Only get out, get out!"

The Caliph dropped his face to his hands. He was tired of this eternal bickering, this quarreling over empires and women, and crazy Franks who went around beating caliphs. He almost wept in his self-pity.

Yussuf al-Zayda had watched this scene from the shadow of an archway. He tiptoed forward now, afraid lest al-Muktafi turn his legs and his arms over to the sharp hooks and hot irons, blaming him for purchasing the Frank.

He whispered, "Lord of Forgiveness, I have prepared your pleasure barge for a trip. You deserve a respite from the cares of state. I have made arrangements for a journey that will take fourteen days and nights."

The Caliph raised his head. "Fourteen days and nights?"

Yussuf al-Zayda groveled. "I took the liberty of purchasing fourteen women slaves, O Son of Allah. Each one of them young, and untouched by man."

Al-Muktafi beamed.

Chapter Fifteen

THE GREAT SILK ROAD that winds through Asia, across the shifting sands of the Kara Khorum, past the stone fire towers of Kashgar and the unknown ruins below Tihwa to the rim of the mighty Gobi and thence on to Taiktu, has its inception in the *sûks* of Baghdad. From these *sûks* eastward, it follows a twisting trail over level, barren plains, skirting the great marshlands to arrive at the foothills of the towering Pusht-i-Kuh escarpments.

In those foothills John of Lincoln rode point for the Princess Shirzade. They had come fast from Baghdad in the dawn hours, galloping with a freshening wind in their faces, the Arab barbs between their knees eager to run. To the big Crusader, the wind that was cooled by the snows from the high gorges ahead and scented by the firs that heaped needles on their slopes was like a welcoming voice. It put new life in him, so that for the first time he began to think of what lay ahead in Samarkand.

There would be honors and riches heaped on him, but they meant little to this man, who was discovering that a strange restlessness ate in him. It was a leaping, live thing that gnawed hungrily, whispering of forgotten memories and ambitions, of high hopes that were now empty mockeries.

He tried to lose himself in activity, toeing his barb into wild gallops between clumps of shrubs and tamarisk, or reining in on the brink of a sheer precipice that looked across a crevasse at a sloping mountain face whose ridges were enameled white with snow. He urged Shirzade on with forced gaiety, racing her along stretches of level limestone, between clumps of tiny purple blossoms, or paused to kiss her breathless on a ledge that looked out over a dozen miles of glacial ice. But that inner uneasiness was always with him.

They rode deeper into the gorges of the Pusht-i-Kuh, filtering their way through the caravan passes, down onto the great gravel steppes that reached away into the desert country. Now there was dry air and midday heat instead of biting cold and winds that stung the flesh.

Their camps were made in the shelter of thornbushes or against sheer rock walls. It seemed that they rode alone through the world, with only an occasional green bush relieving the eternal monotony of brown stone and dun sand. Once they saw a courier riding westward, the yellow scarf that was his badge of office fluttering from his throat.

Now that Samarkand of the high walls grew nearer by the hour, Shirzade was enveloped in a wave of homesickness. She whispered of the arched streets of Bokhara, and of the men who walked those streets with waterskins to wet down the dry dust. She called to mind the silver poplars and black elms that lined the squares of Samarkand, which had once been the city of Alexander the Great. The gold and blue Buddhas, the arched bridges, and the tiled mosques came to life on her tongue.

Her nostalgia bred a mate in the Crusader. He thought of the Holy Lands, and of the fine, high spirit he had known when he fought the Musselmen, and the sadness that had been his because he had been born too late to fight in the armies that had wrested those lands from the paynims.

He grinned wryly. That was a dream he had put away when he took this road with Shirzade. Out of the corners of his eyes he studied her ivory profile, sharp and clear beneath the hood of her gray barracan. Her red mouth and thin arching black brows were engraved somewhere in his heart, and it came to him that he had given up a dream to find reality.

They came at last, after uncounted days of hard galloping and nights of red campfires and cold winds, to the shifting sands of the desert that lies between the Pusht-i-Kuh and the Oxus. As far as they could see, the strange crescent dunes and sand holes of the Kara Kum stretched before them.

"This is the graveyard of caravans, this desert," whispered Shirzade, kneeing her barb closer to the Crusader for comfort. "Here come the jinn and the *ghils,* howling for lives to eat!"

John of Lincoln grinned. "Myths to tell our children!" But her uneasiness added to his own inner restlessness, and it was with frowning face that he rode on.

That night, as if to assuage the gloom that made them its prey, he made her sing to him, interrupting her often to press his lips hungrily to hers. The desert moon silvered her limbs and showed him the bright wonder of her gleaming eyes.

She whispered, "You will be a great lord in Samarkand when I come to the throne, *bagatur*. You will be a ruler of men, and the master of many Mongol archers and Persian swordsmen. With a leader such as you, we will win over many warriors east of the Kara Khitai!"

A pulse hammered in the Crusader's throat. From somewhere deep inside him exaltation welled up, like bubbles from a mountain spring. Mongol archers like Jalagga and Sofodai—little men who fired black arrows fitted with snakebird feathers! *Hai!* If two of them had done so much damage to Imadeddin Zengi's Seljuks, what would a thousand of them do? And with them, dark-skinned men from Samarkand and Bokhara, Balkh and Kashgar, wielding scimitars!

He sat up suddenly. "A Crusade of my own!" he told the night in eager accents. "A Crusade from the East, to hit the infidels where they don't expect it! With the armies in the Holy Lands combined with the archers and swordsmen of middle Asia—*hai!*"

"It pleases you, that thought, Yukhannan?"

"Pleases me? All my life I've dreamed of it! Since I was a boy, polishing the boots of the King of England! Leaning against the bulwark capping of the ship that brought me to these lands! Then finding the Crusade over, with the holy places all won from the Moslems, and nothing left but little fights and petty duelings!"

He went on, gazing down at her pale face. "I thought I'd been born a half century too late. I could not fight for the Holy Land. I could only fight against raiding parties. Now—my own Crusade! Coming back to the lands where I was made exile! Leading an army that will finish off the Saracen threat forever!"

He put his large hands on her and lifted her warm and pliant against his chest. He told her softly, "You made all that possible, little princess!"

With a soft palm she held him off, scanning his glowing eyes with curiosity in her own. "Not in gratitude, Yukhannan! No woman wants to be loved because a man is grateful!"

He laughed deep in his throat. "Daughter of fools! Witch woman! Can you imagine this hunger that is between us to be the result of gratefulness? I'd love you in a hovel. Or like this, in the open, with nothing but two saddles for our home!"

A thunder in the earth shook John of Lincoln to sudden wakefulness. He lay on his back, with the black hair of Shirzade a shawl across his chest as her cheek made a pillow of his shoulder. She was warm and fragrant, relaxed in slumber, and in these first few moments of his sleeplessness, remembering the night, he found her hand and brushed his lips across its soft palm.

Beneath him the earth trembled again, and now the Crusader was wide-eyed, staring straight into the blue desert sky, hearing the distant jangle of scabbard on saddle ring, the pound of many hoofs.

Gently he put the woman from him and stood up.

A great dust cloud was approaching from the west, moving with the speed of a galloping horse. His eyes, trained to such things, estimated the riders that made that cloud at close to a thousand men. He said, "The emir from Damascus—Ramid ibn-Ghazi!"

In that moment of recognition, he knew no bitterness, no anger; only a sense of deadness, of numb shock. The dreams of glory that had brought him into Shirzade's arms, the thoughts that had kept him wide awake after she drifted off to sleep—these were bubbles in a pool, gone at the first brush of a warming breeze.

He knelt beside Shirzade. When her eyes caught the grimness of his face, she whispered, "What is it, Yukhannan?" Her ears heard the coming thunder even as she spoke, and she stood, drawing *tschim* and *salta* about her.

"Unur's man," he told her. "He followed us all the way from Rutba wells!"

He could not know of the hate that twisted and warped the soul of Ramid ibn-Ghazi, the hate that made him sleepless at night and hollow of cheek, that drove him even more ruthlessly than he drove his men. For weeks he had searched the courier trails and caravan routes, sending a score of men north and a score south, and hundreds of others in teams of four to hunt among the rocks of the craggy gorges, lest the man and woman he sought elude him in some hiding place.

Now he gouged his Arab mount with bloody spurs, his lips drawn back to show his teeth. Again and again his hand went to the braided hilt of his scimitar. It had been a long hard chase, but that made this moment all the sweeter. He had known moments of despair, thinking that these two might have swung north or south, or doubled back along the path they had come. Now they stood before him, tiny motes in the vastness of the sands, watching him thunder down at them.

Ramid reined in and his dark hand came up, halting the mail-clad Mamelukes who had followed him from the Desert Gate of Damascus so many months ago. He put his hands on the worn pommel of his dusty saddle and leaned forward, grinning mirthlessly.

"At last," he whispered softly. "At long, long last! Now how shall I kill you, infidel? By steel or fire? Swiftly, in anger, or slowly, in just deliberation, taking thought on what will pain you the most?"

John of Lincoln felt the shudder that ran through Shirzade. She was quivering in despair, too broken even to weep. They had come so far! They had fancied themselves so safe!

As if her tremblings drew him, the Emir put his dark eyes on her.

"The proud princess from Samarkand! The Persian *bayki* who conceives herself too good for a mere emir, and takes an infidel dog in his place! I will teach you to reject Ramid ibn-Ghazi! By the beard of the Prophet, I'll give you to my men, to each and every one of them— after you've watched my campfires cook the skin from this Christian pig!"

Ramid waved a hand and men came forward, leading a trotting pack horse. There was dry wood stored in the wicker panniers on its ribs. The Emir laughed. "All the way from Baghdad that horse has come! Just carrying wood for a fire, a fire that must not burn too fast or too slow. A fire that must burn for some days and nights. And with a different part of the Christian in it every hour!"

Shirzade screamed, with the back of her hand shaking against her cheek.

Ramid ibn-Ghazi leaned forward in his saddle. "Scream louder, Princess. Maybe they'll hear you in Samarkand! It's only half a thousand miles away!"

John of Lincoln put an arm around her and held her tight. He said coldly, "I will fight. It will cost you men to take me."

In the hot triumph that ate at his middle, the Emir threw back his head and poured his laughter to the sky.

"One Christian? Against a thousand men?" he gasped when he could, brushing at his eyes with the back of a wrist. "No, infidel. Your course is run. The hunt is over. Now we'll prepare for the feast."

A dozen men ran for John of Lincoln, their round shields before him. Afraid that Shirzade might be hurt, he had no way of thrusting her aside to draw the scimitar at his hip. The shields came in at him like a fence, crushing him back and away from the lady of Samarkand. A scabbard hooked his ankle and he went down with a weight of men crushing him to the sand.

He rose up, arching his body at feet and shoulders, his arms thrusting, plowing between shields with fingers gripping their edges, tugging them apart. He rolled then, hitting a man with a fist, shouldering another aside until he was on one knee.

For an instant it seemed that he would regain his feet and drag his scimitar from its scabbard. Then the steel ball pommel of a dagger caught him at the temple and he fell forward, face down.

The Emir sighed gently, glancing at Shirzade. "A very ox of a man. He will make a good roast."

They dragged the Crusader to his feet, twisting his arms behind him and lashing the wrists with hempen cording. Rough hands caught at the black leather boot on his left foot, tugging it free.

Flint and steel touched fire to the piled wood and shavings. When she saw the red flames lick upward, Shirzade of Samarkand writhed and wrenched against the hands that held her. Her dark eyes dilated in horror as she watched men carry the Crusader toward those flames. Her red lips parted and her bosom strained at its confining *salta*.

"First a foot," Ramid told her from his saddle height. "We'll cook the naked sole a little, until it blisters." He laughed softly, eying her. "Do you not feel gratitude toward me for letting you watch such a cooking?"

"Pig!" she shouted, struggling against the hands that held her. "Son of a diseased dog and a harlot mother! Brother of rats! You are mad in that mind of yours! Mad with hate and jealousy!"

Ramid leaned from the saddle and brought the back of his hand across her face, cutting her upper lip on her white teeth with the fury of his blow.

A cold voice spoke then from the circle of men about the roaring fire.

"It is as I have always suspected. The men of Damascus are fit only for fighting with a woman, or with a lone man at odds of a thousand to one!"

Jeering laughter rose to paint a flush on the dark face of the Emir as he whirled to stare at the man who dared speak thus to him.

Chapter Sixteen

IMADEDDIN ZENGI stood like a brazen statue, the red fire flames painting his silvered mail with crimson lights. There was disgust and contempt in this man, and he took care to show his feelings to Ramid ibn-Ghazi. His finely chiseled face turned toward the Mamelukes who held the Crusader off the ground, with his naked foot thrust toward the blazing fire.

"Let him go," he said softly.

Ramid screamed, "Your heads will roll if you take his orders! I have a thousand men with me. What can he do, fools?"

Imadeddin Zengi laughed sharply. "Your lust and cruelty blind you, man of Damascus. Look you away from the woman who scorns you and the man you hate, for once. Open your ears to something other than your own voice!"

The Emir straightened in the saddle. His eyes swept the ranks of men who surrounded him. He saw his Mamelukes, but he saw too the Seljuk Turks who rode behind the double-eagle standards. Their scimitars were bare in their hands, and their faces were like brown granite under pointed helms. Moving silently, they had come down on the thousand Mamelukes, wedging them apart, here and there, so that others might follow, until now there were two Seljuks for every Mameluke.

Beyond the rim of the massed men, the army that had followed Imadeddin Zengi all the way from Homs was setting up coned tents. Where the Emir brought a thousand men, the Seljuk war lord brought five thousand.

Almost sobbing in his passion, Ramid ibn-Ghazi turned away from that numbing sight. He panted, "You'll not cheat me of my revenge! If I die, I take you with me!"

Imadeddin Zengi shrugged casually. "What is to be is written in the stars. I seek only the woman. You may have the man."

The Emir hissed. "You can have the woman when I am done with her!" Frustration and hate stole the sanity of the Emir. He almost stood in his stirrups as he shouted, "Only after I take her and give her to a dozen of my men will you get her, Seljuk!"

Imadeddin Zengi put fists to his hips as his hard eyes surveyed this frothing madman. He was a warrior, used to death and killing. Torture too he could understand, when matters of state dictated that a man must loose his tongue. But there was no pettiness in Imadeddin Zengi. His vision was too clear, the scope of his thought too vast, to allow personal feelings to stand in the path on which he put his feet.

Before he could speak, John of Lincoln laughed.

The Crusader put mockery into his mirth. "Six thousand paynims against one Christian and a woman! Good odds!"

Imadeddin Zengi flushed. He whirled toward the infidel, who hung above the ground, still in the hands of the impassive Mamelukes. He said crisply, "Let the infidel dog go. Put him on his feet!"

John of Lincoln lifted his boot and drew it on as the hands fell away from him. He said then, "Let me face your army, man against man! I will fight them two at a time, if those odds taste better to you. If your men can kill me, they can take Shirzade."

Ramid screamed, "Silence that tongue, *nasrany,* or I'll have it burned out!"

Imadeddin Zengi turned his eyes from John of Lincoln to the Emir. He winced in disgust at the madness that sat in the eyes of the Damascus nobleman.

"Perhaps odds of five to one would suit the Saracen courage better," John of Lincoln taunted.

The Seljuk war lord was a proud man. Shame touched him at the thought that he had taken an army to capture one Christian. He opened his fist and closed it slowly in reaction to that shame, even as he looked at the proud ivory loveliness of Shirzade of Samarkand.

This woman was the reason he had crossed the deserts and the mountains. He wanted her as wife to his son Nureddin. But as he regarded her bright eyes and flushing cheeks and the quiver of her high bosom to the emotion within her, he thought, She will never wed my son, or if she does, she will find a way to put cold steel between his ribs before he takes her!

If Ramid ibn-Ghazi had held his tongue, Imadeddin Zengi might have turned his back at that moment and walked away from the fires that awaited the body of John of Lincoln. But the Emir stood in his stirrups and shouted, "Do you think us fools to set you loose with a weapon in your hand?"

The words touched something deep inside the Seljuk leader. He asked bitingly, "Are you afraid of this infidel, man of Damascus, that you should dread such a contingency? He is one man. What can he possibly do?"

"Especially when I'm outnumbered six thousand to one," said the Crusader.

Imadeddin Zengi swore viciously, whirling toward the Crusader. *"Nasrany,* you have said it! One man against one! You will meet a man selected by the Emir, and a man selected by myself. Kill them, and go free, taking the Samarkand woman with you! Die, and I give her to the Emir, to do with as he will!"

Ramid ibn-Ghazi sat frozen. He was outnumbered by the Seljuks. He was well aware that their war lord would have no compunctions about throwing them at him and his men, to satisfy this sudden whim. He moved angrily, and the clang of his scabbard against his spur brought a thought to him.

Perhaps the war lord was right. What sweeter revenge was there than for a man to sink cold steel into the hot flesh of his enemy? The fact that Ramid ibn-Ghazi owned a reputation in the streets of Damascus as a swordsman may have influenced that thought, and allowed it to ferment into decision. The Emir swung down from his Arab horse and began to untie the drawstrings of his *gamis.*

He said, "I myself will meet the Christian dog! When his head rolls from his shoulders, the woman will be mine!"

Imadeddin Zengi turned to whisper to a young officer, "Bring Ayyub to me. Ayyub the Anatolian. He will uphold the honor of the Seljuks."

The Emir was naked to the belt. He drew his scimitar from its scabbard and threw the scabbard from him.

Men fell back in a little circle before these two. The Crusader was big, and his bare chest was thick and his arms were long, but the Mamelukes knew that strength alone would never avail him against a swordsman of such repute as Ramid ibn-Ghazi. They watched through slitted eyes as the Crusader came forward, curving blade held out before him.

The Emir leaped in, his blade making a blue circle in

the light. John of Lincoln countered the stroke and thrust hard. Ramid ibn-Ghazi was not there to take that stroke, but was moving aside and swinging. The tip of his scimitar tore through the flesh of the Crusader's arm.

It was only a shallow cut, but it taught the Crusader caution. The scimitar was not an unfamiliar weapon to him, for he had learned its use in practice with the Knights Templar in Jerusalem. But he needed time in which to remember its feel, and the mobility that was lacking in the long, straight Crusader swords. And so he fought defensively, discovering again that the light blade could be used to parry and slice with a tiny movement of the wrist and hand, rather than the overhand stroke with which he swung the long sword.

They stamped and lunged, darting back when a stroke failed. Their booted feet kicked up sand, and sweat ran in little channels down their chests and backs. John of Lincoln could read the hate that distorted the dark, bearded face before him, but he was not aware that the Emir was backing him around with a flurry of slashes, driving him sideways until his back was to the fire.

He felt the heat of the flames against the back of his legs even as the scream of Shirzade touched his ears. The blue steel arc of the Emir's blade came at him like the darting tongue of some immense serpent and he stumbled, his boots scattering flaming wood and ashes.

John of Lincoln went down, feeling the searing agony of fire on his bare back. Ramid ibn-Ghazi shrieked his triumph and leaped, with his scimitar held out straight before him.

The pain of his blistered flesh and the sight of that blade made the Crusader erupt with frenzy. He threw every muscle of his big body into the wrenching twist that let him elude the point of the scimitar. Its edge caught at his ribs, gashing them, then slid aside to grate downward, deep into the dry sand.

Shock came then to his sword arm, a heavy numbing shock that drove his elbow to the ground and bent his arm aside.

As he fell, John of Lincoln had lifted his own sword. The Emir, lunging in mad triumph, had impaled himself on it. The curving blade pierced him from his navel upward through his chest, so that the point stood out between his shoulder blades.

Ramid ibn-Ghazi rolled back and forth on the sands, sobbing out his life, bloodying the ground, his hands like claws working insanely at the steel that pierced his middle. He screamed once, as the pain filtered through nerves numb with initial shock; and in that screaming, he shuddered and died.

"Yukhannan!"

Shirzade hurled herself forward, pressing her weight to the Crusader as he stood, as if to flood him with her own strength. She was oblivious of the fact that the blood from the flesh wound at his ribs stained her *salta*.

Her hands clutched his forearms fiercely as she stared upward, searching his eyes. "Are you able to go on? Your wounds are so bloody! Yukhannan?"

He held still for a moment, savoring the closeness of her, feeling the wild surge of combat washing away the pain and the tiredness, knowing that this woman would be his if he lived until the sun sank beyond the hills to the west.

"Only one more," he whispered into her fragrant black hair. "One more! Two men dead out of six thousand, and we are free!"

"If Imadeddin Zengi keeps his word!"

A stirring in the ranks of the mailed onlookers caught their eyes. A man was coming through the ranks of warriors, a man with a bald brown head from which a long black topknot hung, a man who towered head and shoulders above the crowd, fully seven feet tall and broad in proportion to his height. In his hamlike hands he carried a great sword, a two-handed scimitar that the paynims called *shamshir*.

"Ayyub," said Shirzade dully.

"Ayyub! Ayyub!" shouted the Seljuks, beginning to laugh and taunt the Mamelukes. "Now we will show the Christian dog what a true paladin is!"

Ayyub came into the great circle, and he lifted his huge *shamshir* and swung it three times in a circle over his head. His beady eyes, like black dots in his immense fleshy face, glittered with cruelty. Only a cloth was twisted at his loins. Otherwise he was naked.

"Come, *nasrany*," he grunted hoarsely. "Come and let me carve you into crumbs with my little darling, my Slaughterer of Infidels!"

At his words the Seljuks howled. Joining them, knowing themselves now leaderless, were the Mamelukes. Striped cloths waved overhead. Someone tossed a helmet high, so that the noonday sun caught and burnished it.

John of Lincoln pushed Shirzade to one side. "Go away, little *bayki*," he told her. "This one is no Ramid, crazy with hate!"

She drew back slowly to the pile of panniers and water-skins that had been their night camp.

The giant Anatolian came in a rush, his bare feet stamping hard, swinging his great blade in a waist-high arc. There was no way to stop that blade. His own scimitar would snap in half were he to try to parry it. As it came hissing sideways at him, the Crusader leaped high in the air, both feet spread wide.

He felt the breeze of that blow as the naked giant tried to swerve his stroke in mid-air, the cold steel just grazing a heel as it went by. John of Lincoln landed on his boots and lunged forward.

Ayyub shook laughter from his folds of fat as he eluded that thrust.

"I'm a cat on my feet, Christian dog! I'm a mountain of meat, but I can move!"

He came in great steps, making the huge *shamshir* whistle in the air, using two massive arms to twirl the steel as if it were a peacock feather. The Crusader gave ground, ducking once, falling backward another time to escape those mighty sweeps.

"Fight, little flea!" grunted the giant.

"Fight! Fight, *nasrany* dog!" echoed the throng.

John of Lincoln used his own blade when he could, not daring to risk it against the wider swathes of that mighty steel, but deftly taking its edge sideways, to slide it from him, or risking the loss of a hand to use the *quillon* as a shield.

Stamping and bellowing, Ayyub forced the Crusader around the circle of sand. Time moved slowly and with dragging feet, and to the Crusader it seemed that for all his life he had fought here on this bit of Asiatic sand, defending himself against this giant of a man whose blade could shear him in two should it land.

Blood ran down his ribs and arm where Ramid ibn-Ghazi had sliced him. Fatigue was a dull roar in his ears. The sun on his wet, naked back was like fire. He stumbled once, and as he slipped, he knew the Anatolian was on him.

The great scimitar came around in a gigantic swing.

John of Lincoln put his own steel up to meet it.

The two-handed *shamshir* snapped the smaller weapon as it might a twig, leaving a scant three inches of blade still fastened to its hilt.

A lean man in a black woolen caftan with red stripes slipped from his saddle, lifting out his *kamis*. Ahmed the Assassin thought this thing had gone far enough. He knew the fabled prowess of the Crusader, and he felt him proof against the crazed emir and the Seljuk. But now the Frank was tired and disarmed, and the Anatolian beast would kill him before he, Ahmed the Assassin, would get a chance at him.

With disgust at his own blundering miscalculation, Ahmed crept toward the inner circle of onlookers.

The Seljuks and the Mamelukes were roaring. Ayyub stood on widespread legs, leering and grinning and nodding at the panting Crusader. He lifted the scimitar high over his head and crept forward, almost on tiptoe.

"Now you die, dog of an infidel!"

John of Lincoln lunged sideways, running. He skipped nimbly ahead of the shouting Ayyub, dodging the swings of that sword, until he was close to the Princess Shirzade.

Then he left his feet in a swooping dive, rolled over once, and came up with a leather sack in his hands. He fumbled inside the sack, gripping cold horn. Then he shook the sack loose and his great spiked ball came free.

Silence hung over the circle of sand as every Saracen eye was caught and held by that spiked knob.

"The *dair azazil!*" whispered the throng.

The spiked ball glittered redly as John of Lincoln swung it high over his head with both hands. The feel of its horn handle between his fingers was bringing back memories of the days when he had swung it in battles from Amman north to Antioch. Those memories were like a drug in his blood, sending new life into his body, filling his veins with the effervescence of fresh hope.

"Come, Ayyub!" he shouted. "Come taste my whirling devil! You had your chance at me. Give me my chance at you!"

The naked giant bellowed and hurtled in. His scimitar swung to meet that spiked globe. Steel clashed and threw off sparks as edge met ball and glanced aside. Again the arms lifted and the weapons whirled and dove.

The throng was breathless, staring. Never before, not even in the days of Jamshid and Harun the Blessed, had such a fight been seen! Eyes were blinded by blue steel and by spike-bristling globe. Men winced at the sound of steel screaming under thudding steel.

Ayyub went back a step, sweat coating his blubber in crystal drops. He fell back another step. This pale *nasrany* was touched by Shaitan! There was no tiredness in him as he swirled the spiked ball around and around and brought it battering down. The shock that went up his arms and into his shoulders as he used the two-handed *shamshir* to parry those smashing blows made the Anatolian shudder.

The giant realized that to retreat further would only expend energy that might be used to batter this mad *nasrany* into the sands. With a shout he heaved his scimitar high and lunged forward.

John of Lincoln came to meet him with the spiked ball whipping down at the end of its chain in a flailing arc of destruction.

The scimitar touched the spiked ball and was brushed aside.

Unchecked, the great steel ball thudded down and into the bald head of Ayyub the Anatolian.

There was no sound from the gathered ranks as the giant stood a moment, dead on his thick legs. Then he toppled, and a sigh lifted from thousands of throats that were parched from excitement.

John of Lincoln dropped the spiked ball and caught Shirzade as she ran to him, burying his face in the thick flood of her black hair. He let her arms cradle him a moment before he drew away.

"We'll see now if Imadeddin Zengi keeps his word to me," he told her.

The Seljuk war lord came walking forward, eyes on the monstrous bulk of his naked champion. He said, "Infidel, never before has there been a fight such as the one this day. Would a *kadi* have told me that one man could defeat Ayyub in single combat, I would have laughed in his beard!"

"Had he told me two hours ago that I would be a free man by sundown, I would have done the same thing," commented the Crusader dryly.

A wry smile twisted the lips of the Seljuk war lord. "I

have given my word, and even my enemies will tell you that I keep it. I will take the Mamelukes with me. None will remain behind to attempt vengeance for the death of their emir."

He gestured his farewells, promising to send his own physician to bind the Crusader's wounds.

The Seljuk war lord was as good as his word. Within two hours John of Lincoln lay bandaged, with his head on a saddle, watching a faint dust cloud move across the horizon. His wounds were painful, but John of Lincoln was used to the bite of wounds. A calmness lay in him, and a deep serenity. The sight of the Princess Shirzade fussing at the campfire made him smile.

He caught her wrist in his hand, drawing her to her knees beside him.

"You move back and forth like a bobbin on a shuttle," he laughed. "What is so important that demands your every interest?"

To his surprise, a flush sat in her ivory cheeks.

"I prepare a feast, *bagatur*," she whispered.

The Crusader frowned. A haunting thought tugged at his memory. "A feast, here? With what? Why?"

"Imadeddin Zengi gave me what I would need. He told me that your wounds would not leave you too weak to chase and—catch me!"

John of Lincoln sat up. "Catch you? Oh!"

She writhed free and stood, eyes glowing as she stared down at him. "Aye, Yukhannan! Catch me after the feasting, to make me your wife according to—"

His hand hooked her ankle, toppling her so that she fell. His arms made her a prisoner and he whispered, "Yes, little *bayki!* Prepare your feast. I find I am feeling very strong and swift of foot. I will run and catch you, as soon as we have eaten."

Chapter Seventeen

THE ROAST MUTTON and date wine was warm in his stomach as John of Lincoln stretched in the red firelight. The cordial that Shirzade had served him bubbled in his veins, until he forgot the ache of his muscles and the occasional bite of his throbbing wounds.

It was pleasant to lie here with the cool wind of the desert night stirring his yellow hair, but it would be more pleasant to run where that wind led, out onto the sand dunes where Shirzade awaited him.

"Give me a little time," she had whispered, ivory cheeks flushing a pale pink as she stood before him. She had brushed her *salta* and *tschim* almost to newness while the meal sizzled over the flames. Her sloe eyes were feverishly bright, and her drooping black lashes did little to hide their hunger.

"Only a very little time," he told her, studying the bare feet she exposed below the gilt foxing of the *tschim*.

She whispered, "I cannot run in my old boots the way I can without them."

He laughed softly, and removed his own footgear.

She knelt to him, and for an instant he felt her mouth against his own. Then she was gone in a flash of bare feet painted henna by the flames, and he lay there, remembering that he must give her time to run.

In the desert darkness the wind died down. As if that were a signal, John of Lincoln came to his feet. He stood like a giant before the fire, in loose black woolen trousers, his chest striped by a white bandage. Then he moved from the flames, out into the blackness of the night.

Ahmed the Assassin lay under the low branches of a desert cactus. His dagger was in his fist as he watched the Crusader move away from the firelight. Now is the time to strike, he told himself, while his eyes are still blinded by the brightness of the fire, before they can react to the darkness. He rose and came forward in one fluid movement, with the sand making little puffs under his slippered feet and the blade of his *kumia* bared.

John of Lincoln did not see him. But the cactus under which Ahmed had hidden himself was possessed of many spikes. Two of these spikes caught in his black caftan with the thin red stripes; caught and held it a moment, before the woolen stuff tore free. The tearing made a jagged sound in the night.

It was that sound that brought the Crusader around in time to see the Assassin's dagger almost at his chest. There was no time to dodge, no time to lift a hand. He was poised on the balls of his feet, leaning forward, out of position for any move but one.

He made that move instinctively. He went forward in the same motion with which he whirled at the sound of the ripping cloth. It meant taking a dagger in the upper shoulder; but if he had stayed as he was, the cold steel would have been in his heart. He felt the graze of the steel, the sudden warmth of blood, and then his hands were lifting to fend off the fanatical killer.

They went rolling and writhing across the cooling sands. Ahmed was like an animal in his lust to kill. His bearded lips whispered panted oaths even as his right arm shook with the insane fury with which he sought to drive his blade downward, for the Crusader had fastened his big right hand around his slim wrist and was holding it motionless in a vise of powerful fingers. Since his dagger was useless to him, Ahmed fought with knee and teeth, driving his bent leg at the Crusader's groin, sinking white teeth into the bleeding flesh of his neck and upper arm.

For months Ahmed had trailed this infidel across a world. For months his every waking moment had been devoted to this act of killing. Now his steel was in his fingers. Now there was Christian flesh within reach of his hand. But this Crusader was fighting with the tireless fury of an animal, threshing and kicking wildly, rolling over and over until he could gain his feet.

Then John of Lincoln was standing, ripping Ahmed from him and throwing him as he might a leech torn from his bloody flesh.

As he fell, Ahmed twisted dexterously and landed on his feet, to come back low, thrusting savagely, with his dagger a splinter of light in the darkness.

John of Lincoln held no weapon in his hand. He had to trust his long arms and big hands not to miss the Assassin in his wild rushes. Once he panted, as the point of the blade sliced the air an inch from his mouth, "So the Turk sent you back . . . to kill me where Ayyub failed!"

Ahmed wasted no breath in denials. Already he had bungled this job. His kind were slayers in silence and in darkness, not fighting men. All he asked of Allah now was a chance to redeem himself by sinking a blade in this infidel, then to flee back to the anonymity of Alamut.

He came in a cloud of sand, snarling curses.

Too late, Ahmed saw the Crusader shift from defense to the attack. One moment there was empty sand and moonlight before him, and the next the Crusader loomed tall above him, and his hands were moving upward in the night. Then those steel fingers were tight about his throat.

Air bubbled wetly in his mouth as Ahmed opened his mouth wide to suck at the desert air. His chest lifted and fell, but no welcome blast of air came down into his heaving lungs. Ahmed tried to scream. In his hate and his desperation he lifted his dagger and thrust it sideways, but the elbow of John of Lincoln was there, thrusting it away.

Those fingers! Merciful Allah! They were like metal cording on his windpipe. He could not breathe. The muscles of his legs were turning to water, and his arms were numb. With dumb surprise, Ahmed saw the empty fingers of his right hand clawing feebly at the face in front of him. He had dropped the *kumia!*

Ahmed knew his eyes were bulging in his head. The night was growing blacker all around him and now there was a roaring lifting up from somewhere deep inside him. Again he tried to claw at the infidel face so close to his own, but his fingers merely brushed at empty wind. Forgotten now was his task of killing. Life for Ahmed became more important than death.

Now the Crusader was standing, swinging the helpless Assassin with savage fury. He shouted, "Go back to Imadeddin Zengi now, slayer of men. Show him how you failed him!"

At the third swing, his neck broke, and John of Lincoln dropped him. As he sprawled limply in death, his torn caftan opened and a little leather sack came loose to spill its contents onto the sand.

An emerald ring lay there, greenly winking up at the Crusader.

Dazedly John of Lincoln bent and put out a hand to the ring. He knew the verdant fire of that stone. He had seen it on the Lady Hodierna many times, in Tripolis and the Krak.

No man of Imadeddin Zengi, then, he thought. An Assassin hired by the Countess of Tripolis to track me across all Asia and kill me!

It seemed to the big Crusader that he could see the Lady Hodierna standing before him, her bosom white and full above the low bodice, her *bliaud* clinging. There was that same sensual smile on her mouth, and that same cold calculation in her dark eyes. He lifted shaking fingers to his brow.

"You sent him all the way out here," he whispered, "just to kill me. Now he's dead and I'm alive, and the last link holding me to your world is gone."

He smiled a little, feeling the hot flood of triumph working in his veins. As if she were really there before him, and not just a fragment from his memory, he went on. "I should be grateful to you for your ambition and your hate. You drove me out of the Holy Land, and into the arms of Shirzade. You wanted to kill me. Instead, you gave me happiness!"

For an instant longer he stood there above the dead body of the Assassin, aware that his brief vision was fading in a shaft of moonlight.

He threw the ring from him and began to run.

John of Lincoln did not run far. He had gone perhaps five hundred yards into the desert when he heard the whisper of metal meeting, and leather creaking, and the slap of a hoof on sand. He paused and stood there, chest lifting and falling, eyes straining to see into the darkness.

They came like shadows from the sands, like a ghostly army walking the paths of Alexander. As far as the eyes could see they moved forward, bulking black in the night. There was a rustling of saddle armor and the creak of lacquered leather, the jingling of headstalls and the faint clang of steel on metal. Men with dark faces under pointed helmets, men with round shields slung to their backs, guiding their horses in a slow walk. There were Mongols with these men, small archers with arrow cases on their hips and powerful bows across their backs, black eyes glittering. His eyes could not see all that host, so far back did it stretch.

The close ranks opened, and a woman came toward him. She wore *chalwar* so fine that her ivory legs seemed garbed in mist, belted with golden disks at her supple waist and again at her slim ankles. Red leather slippers with upturned toes kicked sand puffs as she advanced on him, hips swinging. Chains of pearls hung from her waist, and from the golden breastplates.

Her sooty black hair was coiffured and set with golden teardrops. In the middle of her ivory forehead swung a great red ruby on tiny gold chains. Her eyelids were blued. Below them, her eyes gleamed proudly.

Never before had John of Lincoln seen Shirzade clad as befitted a princess of wealthy Samarkand. His heart hammered wildly under his ribs as she came to a stop before him, perfumed and scented, her ripe red mouth moist and wide.

He said hoarsely, "I did not catch you, *bayki!*"

"You ran, and I came to you, *bagatur*. It is the same thing."

There was tenderness in her eyes, and a deep pride. She turned and gestured at the men who sat their horses like black statues in the night.

"My Lord Yakhannan, these are the warriors of Samarkand, and of the steppes beyond it, sent by my father to bring me home. It seems that he heard some gossip from the caravan traders concerning his missing daughter."

He felt her warm fingers clasp his hand. "All your life, you have dreamed of a crusade. With men like these, you can make such a dream come true!"

John of Lincoln turned to stare westward, as if to gaze for the last time on the sea walls of Tripolis and the marts of Damascus and Baghdad. He saw the stone battlements of the Krak and smelled the cold air off the Pusht-i-Kuh, and heard again the tinkling copper bells of a desert caravan. He had come a long way with this woman whose hand held his own.

He swung back to let his eyes assay the silent horde before him. Then with the Princess Shirzade at his side, he walked toward the warriors of Samarkand, knowing that with their swords behind his banners, he would return someday along the path that had brought him to them.

THE END
of a novel by
Gardner F. Fox

www.ingramcontent.com/pod-product-compliance
Lightning Source LLC
Chambersburg PA
CBHW020648180626
46816CB00003B/1177